EXTREME ADVENTURES

BOOK 5

Spider Bite

"Harry!" I yelled, at the top of my voice. "Climb up and turn the gas off!"

"There's a spider on me," he said.

"Can't you brush it off?" I asked. "Harry, it's only a …"

I stopped short because I'd just remembered something.

Didn't the red-haired woman say a spider had bitten the pilot and made him unconscious? There was only one spider with a bite that bad …

The Sydney funnel-web.

Extreme Adventures

Book 1 – Crocodile Attack
Book 2 – Bushfire Rescue
Book 3 – Shark Bait
Book 4 – Scorpion Sting
Book 5 – Spider Bite
Book 6 – Man-Eater

BOOK 5

Spider Bite

JUSTIN D'ATH

First American Edition 2011
Kane Miller, A Division of EDC Publishing

First published in 2007 by Penguin Group (Australia)

For information contact:
Kane Miller, A Division of EDC Publishing
PO Box 470663
Tulsa, OK 74147-0663
www.kanemiller.com
www.edcpub.com

Library of Congress Control Number: 2010934687

Printed and bound in the United States of America
1 2 3 4 5 6 7 8 9 10
ISBN: 978-1-61067-010-4

For Vincent, the aviator

1

BALLOON CRASH

Jordan saw it first. Or maybe it was Harry. Sometimes I still get them muddled up.

"Holy torpedo!" Jordan (or Harry) cried, eyes nearly popping out of his head.

The other twin and I turned to look.

"What's *that*?" squawked Harry.

A line of tall, Norfolk Island pines grew along the southern end of the park. Looming above them, only the top of it visible, was an enormous red, blue and yellow dome.

"A hot air balloon," I said.

For a moment the twins and I stood in awed silence, watching the balloon float majestically towards us. And towards the trees.

The pilot had better take it up a bit higher, I thought.

Then Myrtle saw it.

Myrtle was our new dog. We got her two days after we arrived in Sydney – a bribe from our parents because none of us wanted to move here after Dad changed jobs. Myrtle was only six or seven months old when we adopted her from the lost dogs' home in Hurstville, but she looked fully grown. Part Newfoundland, part Great Dane, she was so big you forgot she was a puppy – until she saw something to chase.

Poor Harry. He was holding Myrtle's leash when she noticed the balloon. Her favorite game was fetch, and she must have thought the balloon was a giant ball. With a joyous howl, the overgrown puppy took off across the park. So did Harry. He should have let go, but he's stubborn like me, and he held on. Myrtle pulled him along behind her, yelping with excitement and picking up speed with every bound.

Harry stayed on his feet for about a dozen yards, running full tilt, but gradually his whirling legs lost the race, and he went flat on his belly. Myrtle kept going. Straining like a sled dog, she dragged my five-year-old brother across the dew-wet grass, with Jordan and me in hot pursuit.

"Myrtle, *stop!*" I cried, at the top of my voice.

"Here, Myrtle!" yelled Jordan.

We might as well have told our dog to do a headstand. Myrtle was on a mission. She wasn't going to stop until she got the ball. But there was a line of trees in the way, then a road. Even though it was only six-thirty in the morning, this was Sydney, and the roads were already busy with people driving to work.

Myrtle's eyes were fixed on the balloon; she had no idea of the danger.

My eyes were fixed on Harry, and on Myrtle's thick red leash where it emerged from his hands. I had to get my timing exactly right. We'd nearly reached the trees; then it was only a few more feet to the road. Myrtle was about to rush out into the traffic, dragging Harry behind her. Neither of them would stand a chance.

"Harry, *let go!*" I yelled, and dived forward like an Olympic swimmer off the starting block.

Harry doesn't usually listen to me, but this time he must have heard the urgency in my voice and let go. I flew right over him and landed at full stretch in a prickly bed of Norfolk Island pine fronds. It should have hurt, but all I felt was the squashy cord of Myrtle's leash in my fingers. *Gotcha!* I thought.

Jordan caught up and grabbed Myrtle's collar on one side. Harry jumped to his feet and grabbed the other side. We'd stopped her in the nick of time, but Myrtle was still unaware of the danger. Wagging her shaggy tail in my face, she barked excitedly up at the sky. *Please let me go,* she seemed to be saying, *so I can fetch the big ball!*

"It's a balloon, you silly –"

I was interrupted by a loud, splintering crash in the tree directly above us. A shower of twigs, bits of broken foliage and bark fragments came raining down. This was too much for Myrtle. She went totally crazy, wriggling and yelping and leaping up against the tree trunk.

I looked up through the crisscrossed branches and saw a large, rectangular object about fifty feet above the ground. It was the basket from the hot air balloon, stuck in the tree. I *knew* it had been flying too low.

"Is anyone up there?" I shouted.

A faint voice came from inside the basket: "... web ... unconscious ... can't ..."

It sounded like a woman. I couldn't hear what she was saying because of all the traffic noise and Myrtle's carrying-on.

"Hold Myrtle," I said to the twins.

A truck thundered past, so close that we felt its wind. I hesitated. There was no fence to stop Myrtle running out onto the busy road, and she was too big for the twins to control. Next to one of the trees was a water tap attached to a post. I tied Myrtle's leash to it, then turned to my little brothers.

"You guys wait here," I told them.

Hooking my hands around a trailing branch, I swung myself up into the tree.

2

GET OUT OF THE WAY

The basket was the size of a small dumpster. It hung in a nest of tangled foliage and bent branches about three-quarters of the way up the tree. Attached to the basket by a spider web of shiny wires was the balloon itself. Quivering and swaying in the early morning breeze, the huge red, blue and yellow envelope rose a hundred feet above the treetops. It seemed to fill half the sky.

"Help!" the woman called, right next to my ear.

"Are you hurt?" I asked, through the wall of woven cane separating us.

I was directly underneath the basket, looking for a way to climb up and look in without getting myself entangled in wires and prickly branches.

"I think my arm's broken," the woman whimpered.

I tested a branch to see how strong it was, then gingerly transferred my weight onto it. There was an ominous creak. The basket rocked.

"Is there anyone else in there?" I asked.

"Just Anthony, the pilot."

I climbed a bit higher. Now I was level with the basket, no longer below it. But I still couldn't see inside. "Is he all right?" I asked.

"He's unconscious," the woman said. "I was trying to revive him when we crashed."

That explained why the balloon had plowed into the trees instead of flying over them. But it raised another question: Why was the pilot unconscious?

There wasn't time for me to worry about that now. The basket was tilted away from the tree trunk, lying partly on its side with its opening towards the park. To see into it, I had to wriggle out along the branches. They got skinnier and more prickly every inch of the way. As if that wasn't bad enough, the breeze seemed to be gathering strength. The balloon swayed in the sky like an enormous, upside-down punching bag. It rocked the basket (and me) alarmingly to and fro.

I have never been good with heights. I had to stop and take a few deep breaths to calm myself. My palms were sweaty, and my heart rate was maxing out. Then I made the mistake of looking down.

Ohmygosh!

From the ground, the basket had looked about fifty feet up. But looking down, it seemed more like *a hundred* and fifty! My brain recoiled in shock. Every muscle in my body went into lockdown. I clung to the two branches, totally unable to move, as the wind slowly increased in strength and precious seconds trickled by.

"Are you still there?" the woman finally asked.

"Y-y-yes," I gasped.

"Please hurry," she said. "Anthony isn't breathing properly. We have to get him to the hospital. He needs antivenin."

Surprise shook me out of my zombie-like state. *Antivenin.* Wasn't that for snake bites? First I moved one hand, then the other. Then each of my legs. Slow as a sloth, I worked my way along the branches until I was level with the padded basket edge. The balloon's stainless steel burner assembly dangled just above me. I saw a tiny flame inside it – like the pilot light in a gas heater. There were two on-off valves with red levers, and several gas lines that snaked down one of the aluminum support struts and disappeared from view. Being careful not to touch any part of the basket, I peered in.

A red-haired woman sat huddled against two large silver gas cylinders that were strapped to the side of the basket. Her face was deathly pale, and she supported one arm by its elbow with her other hand. Beside her, wedged awkwardly into a corner, lay the man she'd called Anthony. His eyes were closed, and there was a bubble of spit in the corner of his mouth.

"Did a snake bite him?" I asked.

The woman shook her head. "A spider."

At that moment, a sudden gust of wind sent the balloon rolling across the treetops like a massive beach ball. It tugged at the basket, tilting our tree sideways. Timber groaned; wires twanged. I nearly lost my breakfast as the branches supporting me dipped sickeningly towards the park fifty feet below. I could see the twins. One of them – most likely Harry – was aiming a stick up at me like a pretend gun. This was no time for games. *Get out of the way!* I wanted to yell at them, but my vocal cords were frozen.

Suddenly, there was the sound of branches snapping. The basket broke loose. It pivoted around in a semicircle, swinging straight for me. I couldn't let go of the branches to fend it off. All I could do was hang on and watch it get bigger, bigger, bigger …

Whump!

Everything went black.

NEAR-DEATH EXPERIENCE

For a moment I lay still, my eyes scrunched tightly closed, waiting for the pain to kick in. I knew I was badly injured. You can't fall fifty feet headfirst and not wind up in the hospital – or worse.

"Brace yourself," said a woman's voice. "We're about to crash-land."

I opened my eyes. I was lying with my head in the red-haired woman's lap. Above her, framed in a dark rectangle of woven cane, were the gas burners. Above the burners was the huge, brightly-colored nylon envelope of the balloon. I'd fallen into the basket.

But now the *basket* was falling!

I took the woman's advice and braced myself.

Crunch!

That was my second crash-landing in about fifteen seconds. But I felt okay – apart from the dead weight of the unconscious pilot lying on top of me. I pushed him gently to one side and struggled into a sitting position. The woman crouched next to me, clutching her broken arm. We had landed in the park. The basket lay on its side. A few yards away, the slowly deflating balloon sank to the ground like a huge, tired whale.

One of the twins appeared in the mouth of the basket. "That was *wicked!*" he said, which told me it was Harry.

Then they were both there, grinning from ear to ear, as if my near-death experience had been a performance put on for their entertainment.

"I think I'm seeing double," the woman said.

"They're twins," I told her. "Jordan, Harry, help us out of here."

We helped the woman first. She said she broke her arm when the balloon crashed into the trees, and it was very sore. She sat on the ground hugging it while the twins and I went back for Anthony. He was still unconscious. His body lay jammed between the two gas cylinders, as limp as a rag doll, but fifty times bigger. I got Jordan to support his head, while Harry and I eased the unconscious pilot out onto the grass.

As soon as we were all out of the basket, it began sliding slowly away from us across the park. The floppy balloon had filled like a giant parachute in the freshening wind and was dragging the basket along. There was a freeway on the other side of the park, but it was about three hundred yards away, and I didn't think the balloon would get that far before it deflated again.

"Is he breathing?" the woman asked.

I bent over the pilot. "Yes. But he looks pretty bad."

"You'd better get help. But first, put him in the recovery position. Do you want me to show you?"

I shook my head. We'd learned the recovery position in first aid at my old school. I arranged the pilot's arms and legs how I'd been taught, then carefully rolled him onto his side. Perfect.

"Someone's coming," the woman said.

A man hurried towards us. His car was parked under the Norfolk Island pines with its door flung wide-open.

"Can I help?" he puffed. "I'm a doctor."

The woman told him that Anthony needed antivenin. Before she could explain, a loud *whoosh* came from behind us. It sounded like a jumbo jet taking off. We all turned to look.

It took me a few seconds to understand what was happening. The basket was still lying on its side, but it was sliding slowly away from us across the dewy grass. A column of flame ten feet long went boiling up into the balloon. Somehow the gas burner had ignited. Suddenly, the massive nylon envelope lurched up off the ground, dragging the basket upright.

Now we could see what was going on.

"Harry, Jordan, *no-o-o-o!*" I yelled, and started running towards them.

4

LAST CHANCE

They were both in the basket. Jordan looked scared, but Harry was grinning like an idiot and doing a Wiggles dance. I ran after them at full tilt, yelling at them to shut the gas off. I could have saved my breath: Now that the basket was upright, the on-off valve was too high for the twins to reach. Anyway, the roar of the flame made it impossible for them to hear me. It even drowned out Myrtle's barking. I didn't know she was following us until she went charging past me, doing about fifty miles per hour. Behind her, dancing along on the end of her leash, was the tap and a short piece of twisted pipe. She'd pulled it right out of the ground!

The basket grew lighter as the balloon filled with hot air. And the lighter it became, the faster it moved. Pushed along by the wind, it bounced and skipped across the grass five or six yards ahead of me. For a while I'd been gaining on it, but when the balloon reached the long, grassy slope leading down to the freeway, it began to move faster. Six yards stretched to eight, then twelve, then fifteen.

There was a big concrete wall at the edge of the park to keep people off the freeway. It was high enough to stop the balloon – *provided it stayed on the ground.* But if the balloon took off before it reached the wall, it would sail over the freeway and float off towards the city skyscrapers in the distance, taking Jordan and Harry with it.

"Jump out!" I yelled desperately, as the basket slowly drew away from me.

It didn't draw away from Myrtle. Galloping like an oversized greyhound, she caught up with the balloon about forty yards before the freeway wall. Wild with excitement, she began leaping against the side of the basket in a vain attempt to get the giant "ball" that hung in the sky overhead. Then she jumped too high and fell in on top of the twins.

Myrtle weighs about a hundred and fifty pounds. The extra weight slowed the balloon down. I caught up and threw myself across the basket's rim. I wasn't sure what I intended to do. If I'd had my wits about me, I would have reached up and turned the gas off. But I didn't think of it.

"Harry, Jordan, jump out!" I yelled.

Easier said than done. The twins lay in the bottom of the basket, trapped beneath a hundred and fifty pounds of tangled puppy. Myrtle couldn't move. When she'd jumped into the basket, the tap had snagged on the edge, and her legs had gotten caught in the rope.

I made a grab for the tap, but I was too late.

Wham!

We slammed into the wall. The impact flung me off the side of the basket, and my head smacked against concrete. I fell flat on my face on the ground and lay there for a few seconds, seeing stars. The twins' screams brought me back to my senses.

"Sam! Sam! Sam!"

Still groggy, I rolled over and blinked a couple of times. The basket was five feet off the ground, grinding slowly up the concrete wall.

The balloon was taking off!

I was on my feet in a moment. I leapt up and tried to grab the basket, but my fingertips couldn't get a grip on the tightly-woven cane. I crashed to the ground. The basket continued to rise, dragged upwards by the enormous red, blue and yellow balloon, which swayed out over the freeway on the other side of the wall like the giant spinnaker of an America's Cup yacht.

I jumped again, but once more my fingers slipped off.

The basket was over six feet off the ground now, nearly out of reach. There was time for one more jump.

Last chance, I thought.

As I bent my legs to spring, I could hear my little brothers' faint, tearful cries against the dragon's breath roar of the flame.

"Sam! Sam! Sam!"

Summoning all my energy, I jumped.

CAPTAIN AMAZING TO THE RESCUE

As my feet left the ground, I noticed something I hadn't seen before – two wooden skids fixed to the bottom of the basket. At intervals along each skid were narrow gaps between the wood and the cane. They looked just wide enough to get my fingers into. Twisting around in midair like a basketball player doing a reverse slam, I made a desperate, one-handed lunge.

Three of my fingers slid into one of the gaps.

For a few seconds it was touch and go. I dangled by three fingers below the basket, my legs pedaling in the air like a cyclist's, the toes of my sneakers grazing against the smooth concrete wall. Then I swung the other hand up and got four more fingertips into another gap.

I weigh just over a hundred and thirty pounds. The extra load was enough to stop the balloon's ascent. Enough, in fact, to pull it slowly back to earth. The basket, with me dangling below it, scraped back down the wall. My feet touched the ground.

It must have looked funny: this fourteen-year-old kid standing directly under the basket of a hot air balloon, holding it down. But it wasn't funny at all: My little brothers and Myrtle were stuck in the basket. If I let go, I might never see them again.

I felt helpless. The freeway was only a few yards from where I stood, but nobody could see me because of the wall. All they'd see was the huge, colorful balloon billowing over the top; they wouldn't know there was a life-or-death struggle happening on the other side.

I looked back up the grassy slope behind me, hoping to see a jogger or someone else taking their dog for an early morning walk. But the park was deserted. Even the red-haired woman and Anthony and the doctor were no longer in view.

"Help!" I yelled. "Could someone please help me!"

It was no use. Even if there had been someone nearby, they wouldn't have heard me over the roar of burning gas.

The balloon was pulling harder with every passing second. Soon there would be enough hot air inside it to lift me off the ground. My arms began to tremble with the effort of holding on.

"Captain Amazing to the rescue!"

I stuck my head out from underneath the basket. Directly above me, Harry was teetering on its rim. He had climbed out from under Myrtle and was about to jump across to the wall.

"*No!*" I screamed. If Harry jumped, the balloon would be lighter; it would go up in a rush, taking Jordan and Myrtle – and me, if I held on – with it.

I had an idea. "Can you see the gas valve, Captain Amazing?" I asked. Now that Harry had climbed up onto the edge of the basket, he might be able to reach it.

"What?" he yelled.

"Turn the gas off!"

Harry frowned at me for a second, then nodded in understanding and disappeared from view. I clung to the bottom of the basket, my arm and shoulder muscles burning from the strain. I was on my tiptoes now. Slowly but surely, the balloon was winning the tug-of-war. I didn't know how much longer I could hang on. *Hurry, Harry!* I thought desperately. *Hurryharryhurryharryhurryharry ...*

Then something totally unexpected happened. Instead of falling silent, the roar of burning gas suddenly grew *louder*. And up went the balloon. Fast. With me hanging onto it.

I looked down at my dangling feet, and at the ground already three feet below them. *Let go before it's too late!* screamed a little voice in my head. But another part of me was thinking of Jordan and Harry. What would happen to them if I let go?

And then it *was* too late. I was ten feet off the ground and rising. If I let go now, I'd break both my ankles.

Suddenly, there was silence. Not total silence – I could hear the rumble of the freeway traffic – but no more roaring flames.

Harry had turned the gas valves off. Yes, gas *valves*. Plural. The balloon had two burners, not one. The twins had managed to get one of them going to begin with – that's what had caused the balloon to reinflate and blow across the park. But when I'd yelled at Harry to turn it off, he'd operated the wrong valve by mistake and fired up burner number two. That's why the noise had suddenly doubled in volume.

Harry had quickly realized his mistake and shut them both off. But he was too late. Five seconds with both burners running had heated the air inside the balloon to a point where it could lift me off the ground. Even with the gas shut off, it kept going up. With me dangling beneath the basket, hanging on for my life.

We cleared the wall and sailed out over the freeway. I could hear the traffic below me, but I didn't dare look down. The balloon was still rising. My arm muscles felt spongy, and my fingers were losing their grip. I couldn't hang on for much longer.

I was going to die!

Suddenly, a loop of rope came wobbling into view below the basket. "Grab hold!" yelled one of the twins.

Impossible. I needed both hands to maintain my precarious grip on the basket's underside.

"Guys!" I called. "Can you lower it a bit more?"

The rope wriggled down another foot or so.

"Is it tied to something?" I asked, stalling for time. I didn't want to do what I was about to do.

"To the balloon," came the reply.

Swinging my body forward, I speared both feet through the loop, then hooked my legs back so it hitched up under my knees like a rope swing.

Here goes nothing, I thought. And let go.

AIR HORN

If I had a choice between all the careers in the world, the last one I'd choose would be trapeze artist. I don't like swinging by my legs from ropes. In a circus tent – even with a safety net – it would be bad enough. But from a hot air balloon above a six-lane freeway?

This was absolutely the first and last time!

It was probably the last time I did anything, I thought, as I released my grip on the basket.

I'd hoped to grab the rope with my hands, but gravity was too quick for me. I dropped like a bungee jumper for about five feet, then the rope halted my fall with a jerk, flipping me upside down. I lost everything in my pockets, including my brand new MP3 player, but I didn't notice that until later. All I noticed was the view.

Dangling head down from a rope about a hundred feet above the freeway, here's what I saw: the faces of drivers staring up at me through car windshields, their mouths open in astonishment; a man in a four-wheel drive paying more attention to me than the road and nearly sideswiping the taxi in the next lane; a kid wearing a way-too-large crash helmet almost falling off the back of his dad's motorcycle; and ...

Three *big* trucks.

There were two semis and a gas truck. They came speeding along the freeway side by side, taking up all three lanes. The balloon was drifting directly across their path, slowly losing altitude.

"Harry!" I screamed. "Start the burners!"

I don't know if he heard me, but I didn't wait to find out. Jackknifing my body, I grabbed one side of the rope and began hauling myself up like a monkey. Cars swooshed by sixty feet below, creating a windy turbulence that twirled me in circles. A horn blared in the distance. It was an air horn, the kind they have on trucks. I kept climbing. The basket was just above me. One of the twins hung over the side. He stretched a small hand down towards me. The other twin – Captain Amazing – wobbled precariously on the basket's edge, trying to reach the gas valves.

The balloon towered overhead. I could see right up inside it. Something was wrong – a big, circular hole gaped open at the top of the cavernous nylon envelope. A panel had ripped out! No wonder we were losing altitude.

The air horn sounded again, much closer this time. I heaved myself up the rope, hand over hand, until I was level with the bottom of the basket. I was desperately tired, but I kept climbing. My fingers squashed painfully between the rope and the bumpy cane. Almost there! Jordan grabbed my watchband and started pulling. Myrtle was barking. The wailing air horn grew louder, louder, louder. Jordan's grip on my watch was cutting off the circulation to my fingers. I hooked my other hand over the basket's padded rim.

"*Look out!*" yelled Jordan.

There was a sudden push of air against my back, like the wind of a train rushing into an underground station. Instinctively, I tucked my legs up out of the way.

Thump!

The world tipped sideways. With a tortured squeal of cane on stainless steel, the gas truck went sliding beneath the basket like a whale under a dinghy. I held on for my life.

There was a loud *whoosh* and a flash of light.

Shishkebab! I thought. *The tanker has caught fire!*

But there was no huge, end-of-the-world explosion. Instead, the whooshing sound changed to a familiar steady roar, and the flash became a tall column of yellow flame that disappeared up into the balloon. I realized what had happened – Captain Amazing had turned on one of the gas burners!

But he lost his footing when the basket slid off the end of the gas truck. There was a big jolt, and Harry teetered on the basket's rim, arms windmilling to keep himself from falling backwards onto the freeway below. I lunged across the basket and grabbed him around the knees. We tumbled in on top of Jordan and Myrtle.

Swaying drunkenly from side to side, the basket sank down towards the road. The twins, Myrtle and I huddled inside it. Just for a moment, I thought the worst was over.

Then I heard another air horn.

7

FUNNEL-WEB SPIDER

The tour bus looked as big as a train. It came hurtling towards us on a direct collision course. The driver had the morning sun in his eyes; he didn't see us until it was too late. He couldn't change lanes because there were cars on both sides. All he could do was hit the brakes. The tires locked up. With a horrendous squeal, the bus came skidding down the freeway. It wasn't going to stop in time!

I had about three seconds to do something.

I'd already dismissed the idea of firing up the second burner. We were too low, only about three feet above the road. Even with both burners operating, there was no way the balloon would rise high enough to clear the top of the bus before it plowed into us. Our only chance was to go sideways.

Before I'd climbed into the basket, one of the twins had unclipped Myrtle's leash from her collar. The other end was still tied to the tap, which was hooked over the basket's edge. I grabbed the leash in one hand, twirled the tap over my head, and flung it at a passing SUV.

It was a lucky shot. The tap – and the twisted piece of water pipe attached to it – wrapped around the SUV's bull bar like a gaff hook. I hung onto the leash with both hands and gritted my teeth.

The leash snapped taut. It nearly jerked my arms out of their sockets and pulled me halfway out of the basket, but I held on. And both twins held on to *me*, to keep me from going overboard. The SUV swung us around in a wide, gut-churning arc – out of the path of the oncoming bus. The bus hurtled past, all six tires screeching, missing us by inches. I was blinded by black smoke and choked by the smell of burning rubber. Then the air cleared, and I could see again.

The SUV skidded to a standstill. So did the bus – about eighty feet further on. The basket sat crookedly on the SUV's hood, bumping up and down as the balloon pulled at us from above. Only the leash hooked around the bull bar kept us from taking off again. I was sprawled over the side of the basket, half-in, half-out, holding the leash with both hands. One of the twins was still hanging onto me. Myrtle stood with her paws on the edge of the basket, barking up at the balloon. Vehicles were stopping all around us. Tires squealed; horns honked. We'd caused a massive traffic jam that blocked all three lanes for as far as I could see.

A red-faced man got out of the SUV. He looked at the dents the basket was making on the front of his vehicle, then scowled up at me. His lips were making talking movements, but I couldn't hear a word he was saying because of all the other noise.

"Harry, turn the gas off!" I yelled, over my shoulder.

The balloon was pulling really hard now. My arms were shaking from the strain of hanging on. Even though it was the middle of a freeway, we were back on the ground (well, almost) and that's where I wanted us to stay. Why was Harry taking so long?

"Harry!" I yelled, at the top of my voice. *"Climb up and turn the gas off!"*

"There's a spider on me," he said.

Despite the roar of burning gas and Myrtle's hysterical barking, I could hear the fear in his voice. It surprised me. Jordan was the timid one; Harry wasn't scared of anything.

"Can't you brush it off?" I asked.

"It won't let me."

It wouldn't *let* him? Well, duh! "Harry, it's only a … "

I stopped short because I'd just remembered something. Didn't the red-haired woman say a spider had bitten the pilot? Now there was a spider on Harry. It had to be the *same* one. After it bit the pilot, it must have hidden somewhere – behind one of the gas cylinders, or in the weave of the cane – and now it had crawled out again. Onto Harry.

A shiver passed through me. The woman hadn't said anything about the spider, just that it bit the pilot and made him unconscious. There was only one spider with a bite that bad …

The Sydney funnel-web.

THE WORLD'S MOST VENOMOUS

I let go of the leash and hauled myself back into the basket. There were sirens wailing in the distance, and I could hear about two thousand car horns, but I had problems of my own. Or Harry did, and he's my little brother.

"Where is it?" I asked, pushing Myrtle to one side and crouching beside Harry.

He leaned against one of the gas bottles and pointed down at his leg. The large black spider was halfway up his shin. It was a funnel-web, all right – I'd seen them in books. This was a male. They're smaller than females, and much more deadly.

"Will it bite me?" Harry asked.

"'Course not," I said, trying my best to sound upbeat and confident. I didn't want him to panic. He was better off not knowing it was a funnel-web. "Stay still while I brush it off."

But when I brought my hand near it, the spider raised its front legs and the forward part of its body and aggressively bared its fangs at me. Now I understood what Harry meant when he'd said it wouldn't let him brush it off. This was one scary spider! And a dangerous one, too – according to the books I'd read, the male Sydney funnel-web is the world's most venomous spider.

The basket swayed one way, then the other. I had to steady myself against the second gas bottle. The chorus of car horns no longer surrounded us, but floated up from below. We were flying again. When I'd let go of the leash hooked around the front of the SUV, the balloon had taken off and gone sailing away on the wind. Who knew where we'd end up? But I would worry about that later. First I had to deal with the deadly spider on Harry's leg.

"Why don't you squash it?" asked Jordan.

"Because it's on my leg, stupid!" said Harry. "If Sam squashes it, it'll bite me."

"How can it bite you if it's dead?"

"*Before* it's dead, stupid!"

"Shut up, you two!" I snapped. Myrtle sensed my nervousness and licked my face. I elbowed her aside. "Jordan, make yourself useful and hold Myrtle."

The funnel-web started crawling. Very slowly, it crept up towards Harry's dirt-smeared knee.

"It's going into my shorts," he breathed.

I couldn't let that happen. Once it was under his clothing, the danger would be much worse. If Harry moved the wrong way, and the fabric pushed against the funnel-web, it would bite him for sure.

"Stay absolutely still," I said.

Moving both hands slowly, I gripped the shorts on either side of Harry's leg and pressed the hem against his knee, just above the spider. It reared up again, swiveling its deadly fangs towards my right thumb, only an inch away. I wondered how fast funnel-webs could move, and whether they could jump. But I forced myself to remain still. Any sudden movements, and the spider might bite my little brother.

After what seemed like an hour, but was probably less than fifteen seconds, the funnel-web resumed its slow, hairy-legged crawl up Harry's leg. Just as I'd hoped, it crept between my trembling hands onto his shorts. As soon as all eight legs were on the fabric, I gently changed my grip.

"Get ready to lift your feet," I told Harry. "I'm going to slide your shorts down very slowly with the spider on them."

It was a good idea. But it didn't work. When the spider felt Harry's shorts stretch tight, it went scuttling up under his T-shirt and out of sight. Harry didn't move, though his eyes grew to nearly twice their normal size.

"Where is it?" I asked. My inclination was to whisper, but I had to speak loudly because of the gas burner roaring away above our heads.

"On my tummy," Harry said, through clenched teeth.

"High up or low down?"

"Near my bellybutton."

I gingerly hooked my fingers under the hem of his T-shirt. "Harry, I'm going to lift your T-shirt, okay? And then I'm going to get the spider off you."

I tried to sound confident. I certainly didn't feel it.

Slowly, I lifted Harry's T-shirt, being very careful not to brush any part of it against his skin. Or against the funnel-web. There it was, crouched in the middle of Harry's stomach. The big, ugly spider didn't move, but its eight beady eyes watched me lift the T-shirt right up to Harry's chin.

"Hold your shirt up like this," I said. "And whatever you do, don't let it fall back down."

Harry did as I said. By now he'd sensed how scared I was, and he looked scared, too. There were goose bumps all over his arms and body. The funnel-web still hadn't moved.

I looked around. "Jordan, is there anything in here that's loose? A piece of wood or something?"

"There's a fire-putter-outer."

He meant the fire extinguisher mounted on the opposite side of the basket. It looked a bit big for what I wanted, but it would have to do.

"Or … the phone," Jordan said, noticing my hesitation.

"What phone?" I asked.

Jordan looked guiltily at his twin brother.

"Show him," Harry muttered.

Jordan's face turned red. He reached behind one of the gas cylinders. "We weren't going to steal it …"

"Just give it to me!" I held out my hand

impatiently for the phone. The red-haired woman or Anthony must have dropped it. We could call for help. But first I had to get the funnel-web off Harry, and a phone might do the trick.

It wasn't a phone, it was a two-way radio. Which made it better for my purposes, because it had a stumpy black aerial – perfect for a spider to climb onto.

But the spider didn't think so. Instead of crawling onto the aerial when I positioned it like a climbing ramp in front of it, the funnel-web reared up and bit it. I tried a second time, and once more the spider struck the aerial with its large, curved fangs. I could actually see tiny smears of deadly venom on the black plastic. *Better on the aerial than in Harry's bloodstream,* I thought, and poked the spider again.

This time I got the reaction I wanted. Instead of just biting it, the funnel-web wrapped its elongated pedipalps and several black hairy legs around the aerial. When I gently pulled back, the spider came, too. It was dangling from the aerial, no longer on Harry's stomach.

Slowly, I stood up, being super careful not to shake the spider off, then held the radio out over the side of the basket. The view gave me a bit of a shock.

We were about three hundred feet off the ground, sailing over orange rooftops and blue swimming pools and miniature cars parked in driveways. A tiny dog ran in circles in its backyard, barking up at us. Myrtle heard it and nearly jumped out of the basket.

"Jordan, keep her under control!" I snapped.

"I'm trying to," he said, "but she's too big."

"Give him a hand, Harry."

In the few seconds that I'd been distracted by Myrtle, the funnel-web had crawled up the aerial onto the radio. It came scuttling towards my hand. I gave the radio a shake, but the spider hung on. I shook it again, harder this time. Three of the spider's eight legs came loose for a moment, then it found footholds in the speaker holes and made a determined rush at my fingers. I juggled the radio from one hand to the other. Now I was holding it by the other end, and the spider was crawling away from me.

Suddenly, the radio crackled into life. "Retrieve One to VH-JZY. Come in, please."

I got such a surprise that I nearly dropped it, spider and all. And it would have been better for everyone if I had.

"Retrieve One to VH-JZY," the squeaky voice

repeated. "Are you receiving?"

I glanced up at the balloon. Written in bold black letters across one of the yellow panels was its registration number: VH-JZY. The person on the radio was calling me!

SPIDER BITE

"Hello, Retrieve One, this is VH-JZY," I said. "But I'm not Anthony, the pilot. He got bitten by a funnel-web spider, and he's on his way to the hospital. My name's Sam Fox. I'm in the balloon with my two little brothers. We don't know how to land it. Can you tell us what to do?"

The instrument crackled again. "Retrieve One to VH-JZY. Are you receiving? Over."

"Hello!" I shouted. I couldn't bring the radio any closer to my face because of the funnel-web. It had turned around and was crawling back towards my fingers. I had to change hands again. "Can you hear me, Retrieve One?"

"VH-JZY, come in, please," said the voice on the radio.

Whoever it was couldn't hear me. There must have been a transmit button to press when you talked. But the funnel-web was crawling across the buttons, so I couldn't get to them. Stupid, dumb spider! I gave the radio a really violent shake, and this time the spider let go. But it flicked *up*, instead of down. And the wind blew it straight back at my face.

Shishkebab! I ducked out of the way just in time. The big black spider went cartwheeling over me.

And landed in Jordan's hair.

This time I didn't hesitate. I spun around and used my hand to flick the funnel-web off my little brother's head.

Snap! went Myrtle's big, rat-trap jaws. She chewed a couple of times, then swallowed and licked her chops. I wasn't worried about her; I knew that dogs weren't affected by funnel-web poison.

"Eeeew!" said Harry.

I crouched next to Jordan. "Are you okay?"

He rubbed his head and nodded. But there were tears in his eyes. "That hurt," he said. "Why did you hit me?"

"Because the spider was on your head, dummy!" said Harry.

"I had to get it off you," I explained.

Jordan stopped rubbing his head, looked at his hand, and promptly started crying.

"What is it?" I asked.

Wordlessly, he held up his hand to show me. There was a red smear on one fingertip. Blood.

I parted Jordan's hair and found a tiny graze on his scalp. No bigger than a pin prick, it could have been caused by one of my fingernails – they needed cutting. But there was another explanation for the broken skin, one that I didn't want to think about.

"Jordan, how are you feeling?"

"O-o-okay," he sniffed, rubbing his head again.

"Does it hurt?" I asked.

"Little bit," he said. He was speaking softly, and it was hard to hear him because of the gas burner. "Did the spider bite me?"

"No," I said, hoping I was right. "It was my fingernails. Look how long they are. I should chew them like you do, hey?"

Jordan gave me a brave, little smile, and I patted him on the shoulder. I tried to remember what you were supposed to do for spider bites. A pressure bandage was out of the question – you can't stop the flow of blood to someone's head.

I had to get Jordan to a hospital. If it was a funnel-web bite and not a fingernail scratch, he needed antivenin. But first I had to land the balloon. I would call Retrieve One – they must have been the balloon's ground crew – and they'd tell me how to land it.

Where was the two-way radio? It was no longer in either of my hands. With a mounting sense of unease, I searched every corner of the basket. The radio was nowhere to be found. Uh-oh. There was only one other place it could be.

I looked over the side of the basket. We were no longer flying over houses and backyards. Instead, there was a series of long, grassy lawns surrounded by sand traps and trees. A golf course. It wasn't even seven in the morning, but there were already golfers down there. Three tiny figures stood on a putting green directly below me. One was lining up his shot, while the other two stared up at the passing balloon.

"Help!" I yelled, at the top of my voice, waving my arms.

On either side of me, the twins yelled and waved

their arms, too.

And Myrtle barked.

But the golfers couldn't hear us. We were too high, and the roar of burning gas was too loud.

"You idiot, Sam!" I said, clapping myself on the forehead. I reached up and switched off the burner valve.

After the constant roar of the flame, the sudden silence came as a shock. Even Myrtle seemed surprised. She stopped barking. All we could hear was the soft creaking of the basket, the gentle sigh of the wind in the support wires, and the rustling of the huge, nylon envelope that carried us majestically through the sky. It was strangely peaceful. And weird to think we were in the middle of the largest city in Australia.

"Help!" I yelled down to the golfers. "Call an ambulance! We need funnel-web antivenin!"

One of the golfers gave us a friendly wave. They couldn't hear me. We were still too high.

Why weren't we losing altitude? I'd turned off the gas. I looked up into the cavernous interior of the balloon and saw the reason. There was no longer a big, circular hole at the top, so the hot air was still trapped inside. It didn't make sense. How could there be a panel ripped out of the balloon one minute, then the next time I looked up it was fixed? Had I imagined it?

"Harry, Jordan, did you guys notice a big rip in the balloon just before we crashed on the freeway?"

"It came open when you climbed the rope," said Jordan.

"And it closed when you got into the basket," said Harry.

A rip that opened when you pulled a rope, then closed when you let go of the rope? I looked at the rope the twins had lowered to me. One end was fixed to the edge of the basket. The other end went up inside the balloon, all the way to the top. I gave it an experimental tug, and the crown of the balloon opened like a giant camera lens. The penny dropped. It wasn't a rip; it was a vent to let the hot air out. When the pilot wanted to land, he simply pulled the rope.

Sweet!

I held the vent wide-open, and sure enough, the balloon began to float gently down towards the sprawling, green fairway two hundred feet below. The golf course's tree-lined boundary was about five hundred feet ahead. Beyond it, the sprawl of the suburbs stretched all the way to the towering concrete and glass skyscrapers of Sydney in the distance. The tops of the tallest buildings were lost in the clouds. That surprised me. The sky had been mostly clear when the twins and I took Myrtle to the park for her early morning walk. The wind must have pushed the clouds up from the south.

The wind was pushing us towards the city, too. If we didn't make it to the ground in the next five hundred feet, there'd be nowhere to land. I tugged on the rope even harder, trying to accelerate our rate of descent, but the hole was open as wide as it would go.

It was going to be close, I thought, gauging the angle of our descent against the distance to the end of the golf course. Too close for comfort. But I reckoned we were going to make it. Just.

Jordan tapped me on the arm. "Sam, I don't feel so good," he whimpered.

He didn't *look* so good, either. His face was deathly pale, and he was shivering so hard his teeth rattled. There went my fingernail theory. Jordan had been bitten by a Sydney funnel-web spider, end of story.

It might be the end of Jordan, too, if I couldn't get him to the hospital in a hurry.

"Sit down," I told him. Apart from pressure bandages and antivenin, the only other useful thing I could remember about treating snake and spider bites was to keep the victim still and calm. He would be safer in the bottom of the basket anyway, if we made a bumpy landing.

"Harry, pull Myrtle around the other side of the gas bottles so Jordan can sit down."

"The spider that bit him," Harry said, as he wrestled Myrtle out of the way, "it was a funnel-web, wasn't it?"

"No, it wasn't," I lied. I didn't want Jordan to panic.

"I heard you tell those men playing golf it was a funnel-web."

Shut up, Harry! I thought. "We don't even know for sure if it bit him," I said unconvincingly. "Jordan, how are you feeling?"

"C-c-c-cold," he whimpered, sitting hunched over in the corner next to my feet.

"Sydney's always cold," I said lightly, trying to make a joke of it. "We aren't in the Northern Territory anymore."

I wished we were back there. I wished we'd never moved. If only Dad hadn't gotten the principal's job at Sydney Grammar, then none of this would have happened.

Harry tapped me on the elbow. "Sam, are we going to hit those wires?"

I looked where he was pointing.

Shishkebab! Crossing the fairway directly in our path were eight high-voltage power lines.

In roughly sixty seconds, we were all going to be fried.

KABOOM!

Power lines, I've since learned, are a balloonist's worst nightmare. They are the first thing a pilot looks for when approaching a landing site. And the *last* thing he sees if he's careless.

The tall, metal pylons on either side of the golf course should have been a dead giveaway, but I wasn't a pilot, and this was my first time in a balloon. All I'd been interested in was the fairway. The long, grassy strip had looked like an ideal place to land.

Because of my inexperience, I had set us on a fatal collision course. We were still a hundred feet above the ground – too high to jump to safety – and the wind was pushing us steadily towards the high-voltage wires.

We had to gain altitude. Fast.

I let go of the vent rope and turned both burner valves on full. *Whoosh!* Two columns of fire shot up into the balloon. The air quivered with radiant heat. The basket trembled. I looked up and saw the vent closing, then I glanced across at the power lines. They were barely forty yards away and getting closer every moment.

Below us, two women got out of their golf cart to watch us pass overhead. One of them waved. Harry waved back, but I had other things on my mind. Despite the roaring burners, despite the double dose of heat being blasted into it, the balloon was still losing altitude. I'd let out too much hot air when I'd had the vent open. The ground came closer and closer. Thirty yards became twenty, then fifteen. Another ten yards, and we could jump. We might break an ankle or a leg, but it was better than being fried in the power lines.

A man came running up onto a small, grassy mound not far ahead. It was a raised area where golfers teed off for the next hole. He started yelling at us and pointing up into the sky with his golf club.

I couldn't hear him because of the burners, but it was pretty obvious he was warning us about the power lines. I shook my head to show him I was helpless to do anything about it. We were at the mercy of the wind. It seemed to have died down a bit since we'd descended to treetop level, but it was still pushing us steadily towards the wires.

I dragged Jordan to his feet. "We've got to jump!" I yelled.

Jordan seemed dazed, as if he didn't know what was going on. He took one look over the side and shook his head. I tried to lift him, but he fought and struggled. He muttered something about Myrtle.

"We can't do anything about her," I said, trying to block my mind to what would happen to Myrtle in about twenty seconds – and to us, too, if we didn't abandon ship. "We've got to save ourselves!"

Then I felt the basket floor push up against my feet. The balloon had started to rise at last. But was it too late? Would it climb high enough to avoid the power lines before the wind drove us into them?

"Will I jump?" Harry asked uncertainly.

He'd climbed up onto the edge of the basket and was crouched there, looking down. Hesitating. We were right over the grassy mound. Although we'd started to rise, the elevated tee was only about fifteen feet below the basket.

The man on the ground dropped his club and opened his arms to catch Harry.

"Go, Captain Amazing!" I yelled, and gave him a push.

Harry let out a loud "Whoopeeeeee!" that lasted all the way down. I didn't see if the man caught him because I was too busy lifting Jordan up to drop him out, too. But when I looked over the side, I quickly changed my mind. The loss of Harry's weight had caused the balloon to shoot upwards. Already we were about thirty feet off the ground, too high to jump. Jordan and I were stuck in the basket with Myrtle. All three of us would share the same fate. Thirty thousand volts. It was going to be quick.

I slumped down with Jordan in the bottom of the basket. We clung to each other. *At least Harry made it*, I thought. The golfer would have caught him. Even if he didn't, it would take more than a fifteen-foot fall to put an end to Captain Amazing. Myrtle licked my face, and for once, I didn't push her away. I tensed myself for a huge bang, a blinding flash, and oblivion.

Twang! The basket jerked and tipped. Jordan, Myrtle and I rolled around in the bottom.

This is it! I thought.

But there was no explosion. The basket was jiggling up and down like a tea bag and leaning over at a sharp angle, but there was no crackle of electricity, no flames. I steadied myself against one of the gas bottles and dragged myself up to the padded edge to look out.

Shishkebab! We were snagged on the top-most wire. The thick, metal cable had become caught around the bottom of the basket. It pulled us one way (down), and the balloon pulled us the other way (up). We bounced like a yo-yo. Every time we went up, the wire stretched tight as a guitar string all the way to the two distant pylons. Every time we came down, it nearly hit the wire below.

If the two wires touched, there would be a 30,000 volt short circuit ...

Then, *kaboom!*

UH-OH!

I had to free us from the wire. But how? It had 30,000 volts running through it. The fire extinguisher wouldn't work; it was too smooth and slippery. *And* it was made of metal – it might cause a short circuit. I would have to use my feet.

I know that sounds crazy, but I had no other options. Besides, Auntie Erin's boyfriend is an electrician, and he told me that you can actually touch a live wire and not be electrocuted if you aren't standing on the ground, or touching something that's connected to the ground. It seemed like a useless piece of information when Alby told me, but now it might just save Jordan, Myrtle and me from being fried to a crisp.

I wasn't standing on the ground, and the balloon wasn't connected to anything except the wire. So, according to Alby, I wouldn't be electrocuted. Hoping with all my heart that he had his facts right, I swung myself up onto the edge of the basket and swiveled around so my top half was inside, and my feet were dangling out. I had to hold on tight because the basket was bouncing all over the place.

"Sam, what are you doing?" Jordan asked weakly. He had one arm around Myrtle's neck and was looking up at me with big, scared eyes.

"I've just got to check something out," I said lightly. The less he knew, the better. He'd been bitten by a funnel-web spider and was supposed to be staying calm.

I felt anything *but* calm as I looked over my shoulder and saw the golf course far, far below. Some tiny people were down there looking up at me. The smallest one was waving. Gritting my teeth, I lowered my sneakers until they were an inch or two above the thick gray cable. Then I hesitated. *Alby, you'd better be right,* I thought, and lowered my feet, slowly, until ... they ... finally ... touched.

Nothing happened. I was standing on the wire, and I was still alive!

The wire was alive, too. I could feel a tickly buzz through the rubber soles of my sneakers as 30,000 volts hummed beneath them. The wire was wrapped around one corner of the basket, snagged in a deep groove – it must have sawed its way into the cane when we crashed into it. When I tried pushing with my feet, the wire wouldn't come loose.

I clung to the rim of the basket as the balloon lifted us upwards. Then I held on as we swung back down. The wire pressed against my feet. This was insane. There I was, two hundred feet off the ground, standing on a wire, with only the thickness of my sneakers' worn, rubber soles between me and 30,000 volts!

I waited for three more swings, counting off the seconds from the basket's lowest point to its highest, until I had my timing exactly right. Then, halfway up the next swing, in the moment when the wire had the least pressure on it, I pushed against it with all my might.

Twang! The wire shot out from under me like a released bow string. I nearly went with it, but luckily I was clinging tightly to the edge of the basket. My swinging feet came perilously close to hitting another wire, then the balloon pulled me up and away.

The basket had been caught on the wire for over a minute. During that time, both burners had been going full blast. Suddenly freed, the huge, overheated and over-inflated balloon shot up like a cork under water, so fast that I had trouble dragging myself back into the basket. I went in headfirst and landed awkwardly between Jordan and Myrtle.

"What happened?" Jordan asked, in a small, shaky voice.

I pushed Myrtle's wet nose out of my face and sat up. "We got tangled in some wires, but I managed to get us free."

"Is Harry okay?"

"He's fine," I said, remembering the tiny figure waving to me. "What about you?"

"I'm still a bit cold."

Even with the roar of the two gas burners, I could hear his teeth chattering. I struggled out of my T-shirt. "Here, Jordie, put this on."

I helped him into it. Two big, wobbly tears dribbled down his cheeks. "Am I going to die?"

"Of course not."

"Harry said the spider was a funnel-web. He said you die if they bite you."

Harry should learn to keep his mouth shut, I thought. "They've got medicine now. It's called antivenin. It'll make you good as new."

"Are we going to the hospital to get it?" asked Jordan.

I almost ruffled his hair, then remembered the spider bite on his scalp and touched him on the cheek instead. "That's exactly where we're going, bro. We'll land on the roof!"

I wondered if that were possible. There were a lot of hospitals in Sydney, and I knew some of them had heliports on their roofs. A good pilot might be able to put a balloon down on one, provided the wind was favorable. I scrambled upright and looked over the side of the basket.

Ohmygosh! We were *soooooooo* high! The houses looked no bigger than bits of Lego. They were slightly hazy because a thin layer of misty air was passing beneath us. The balloon was almost in the clouds. And it was still going up. I reached above me and switched off both burners.

There should have been almost total silence. The

only sounds I *should* have heard were the creak of the basket and the whisper of the wind. But there was another noise, a high-pitched, whistling sound that grew louder with every passing second. It was impossible to tell which direction it was coming from.

I turned in a slow circle, searching for the source of the noise. Straight ahead was the city center, looking much closer than before. The top of Centrepoint Tower poked into the clouds. In the other direction was Botany Bay and the airport. I could see a big runway lined up almost exactly with our present position. *It's a pity we're not in an airplane,* I thought. I could fly down and land.

Then I had another thought: *Uh-oh!*

The whistling sound increased to an ear-splitting roar. I glanced over my shoulder, and my worst fears were confirmed. Five sets of enormous wheels descended out of the clouds, followed by a huge white shape that stretched from one side of the horizon to the other. It was a 747 – a jumbo jet – on its final landing approach to Sydney Airport.

And we were directly in its path.

DEATH ROLL

A fully-laden jumbo jet weighs two hundred tons and its landing speed is 110 mph. It can't slow down without stalling, and it needs about a mile of clear air ahead of it to change direction. We were about three hundred yards ahead of it. The pilot couldn't do anything to avoid a collision.

It was up to me.

I hit both burner valves, cranking them wide-open. Then I shouted at Jordan to hold on and grabbed one of the burner struts for support.

The jumbo jet came thundering towards us, its huge engines churning the air like four massive blenders. It looked as big as a shopping center. It was the scariest sight I had ever seen.

I've been attacked by giant crocodiles, bitten by a blood-crazed tiger shark, stalked by starving dingoes and tossed by a mad, old bull, but on a fear-factor scale, none of them gets a perfect score. Only that 747 earns the full ten points. Because you can't defend yourself against a jet airliner. You can't whack it with a buffalo bone, or deliver a power *shuko* to its eye, or fight it off with burning spinifex, or show it who's boss with a stick and a rope. You can't do *anything* to protect yourself. All you can do is hang on and pray.

But there wasn't time to say a prayer. The jumbo jet was coming too fast. No way was it *not* going to hit us!

I actually saw into the flight deck. Two startled faces – the pilot and copilot – gawked at me through a cockpit windshield that grew bigger and bigger, then shot past almost close enough to touch. The huge white fuselage followed, in a flickering blur of windows like a speeding train going past. Next came a wing the size of a football field – missing the bottom of the basket by no more than a yard – and finally the tail, its flying kangaroo emblem as big as a billboard. Then the jumbo jet was gone.

Made it! I thought.

And that's when the fun started.

As the enormous jet thundered into the distance, the full blast of its four massive, turbofan engines suddenly hit us. The engine wash from a 747 is equivalent to a force twelve gale. It's enough to uproot trees and knock over small buildings. No balloon ever made was designed to fly in winds like that.

It was the wildest ride I've ever experienced. Ten times as bad as anything at the theme parks on the Gold Coast. I couldn't see what was happening because the jet wash blew me into the bottom of the basket with Jordan and Myrtle. But I could see what was above us: the ground! It didn't make sense. Why were those tiny toy houses, toy cars and toy streets *above* the balloon?

Then I figured it out: We were upside down. The balloon was looping the loop!

I thought we were going to fall out, but the G forces pinned us to the basket floor. If Harry was there, he probably would have raised both arms above his head and let out one of his Captain Amazing yells. But there's only one Captain Amazing, and Jordan and I are both scared of heights. We remained grimly silent, holding on to each other as the balloon continued its crazy somersault. Over it went in a seemingly endless, dizzying, gut-churning death roll, until the sky appeared above us again.

But the nightmare ride wasn't over yet. The balloon swayed back and forth like a giant pendulum for another twenty or thirty seconds. Each swing was slightly less-pronounced than the one before. Then we finally settled back into a balloon-up-basket-down position, and the only movement was that of the wind pushing us gently along.

"Phew!" I said, giving Jordan a gentle squeeze and patting Myrtle with my other hand. "Wasn't that fun, guys?"

"I think I'm going to chuck," Jordan said.

FLYING SAUCER

I helped Jordan to his feet and supported him while he hung his head over the side of the basket. He was shivering violently. I was the one who should have been shivering – I was bare from the waist up. Jordan was wearing two T-shirts – mine and his – yet he was still cold. It must have been because of the spider bite.

"How are you feeling?" I asked.

He coughed a couple of times, but didn't throw up. "A bit better now," he whispered.

"Do you want to sit down again?"

Jordan shook his head. "Where's the ground gone?"

I looked over the side. There was nothing below us but clouds. Nothing in any direction but clouds. We were flying blind.

"Um, down there somewhere," I said uneasily. I didn't like not being able to see. "I think I'll take us down a bit."

I reached up to turn off the burners, but stopped halfway. Huh? The gas was already off. Or the flames were, anyway. The burners still made a loud hissing sound, but instead of fire coming out, two jets of spray squirted up into the balloon and dissolved in a swirl of white mist. The engine wash from the jumbo jet must have blown the flames out. I desperately tried the valves, turning them off, on, off, on, off, on, but the spray refused to burn. The pilot lights had blown out, too.

If only I'd used my brain. If only I'd looked more carefully. There was a little red ignition button underneath each burner. All I had to do was press them. But I was in a panic, and blind to what was right there in front of my eyes.

Matches! screamed a little voice in my head. *I need matches to light the burners!*

There weren't any in the basket. There was a

fire extinguisher, which was kind of ironic, but no matches. We were in deep trouble. A hot air balloon without working burners soon becomes a cold air balloon. And a cold air balloon won't fly; it'll crash.

I had already crashed once that morning. Dropping roughly fifty feet from the Norfolk Island pines had been bad enough. But dropping three thousand feet? It was going to be nasty. Probably fatal.

"Jordan," I said, looking my little brother in the eye, "if something happens to me and you get rescued, promise me you'll tell them about the funnel-web spider."

He shuddered. "What will happen to you?"

"Nothing," I said. "But just in case."

I looked over the side of the basket. All I could see were clouds. Were we high enough? A plan was forming in my mind.

Before we went into the clouds, the balloon had been drifting in a north-easterly direction. Straight towards the center of Sydney. Provided the wind didn't change, and we stayed in the air long enough, we would pass directly over the city. And then drift out over the harbor.

We could land there, I thought. I could open the vent and put us down in Sydney Harbor. It would be a nice, soft landing. There'd be no freeways to worry about, no trees to get stuck in, no power lines, no train tracks, no steep rooftops, just a nice, gentle splash-down on the water. I wasn't worried about drowning because someone would rescue us – there'd be ferries on the harbor, even this early in the morning; people used them to go to work. Besides, the basket would probably float.

But first we had to *reach* the harbor. Were we even *moving*?

When you're in a balloon, and the balloon is in the clouds, you have little or no sense of movement. Unless your flight path brings you into close proximity with something very tall.

At first it looked like part of the sky, a slight thickening in the murk ahead. Then it became an eerie yellow shadow that still looked more like clouds than anything solid. Finally it morphed into an enormous golden cylinder that seemed to float in the air with no visible means of support.

"It's a UFO!" Jordan gasped.

I didn't contradict him. It *did* look like a UFO.

Myrtle seemed spooked by it, too. Standing up with her front paws resting on the edge of the basket, she bared her teeth at the strange object and growled.

"Take it easy," I said, holding her by the collar in case she tried jumping out. "It's only Centrepoint Tower."

We drifted slowly past, so close that I saw our reflection in the four tiers of golden windows around its huge, circular turret. And I noticed something else: The windows seemed to be going up. Which meant we were going down.

Suddenly, we dropped below cloud level.

I looked over the edge of the basket. Big mistake. Toy skyscrapers pointed up at us like gray rectangular fingers. Rows of traffic nudged through the deep canyons between the buildings. Pedestrians looked like ants. Jordan made a gagging noise, like he really was being sick this time, and sank down onto the basket floor. My stomach felt weak, too, and so did my knees. I felt like I was about to pass out.

Stop looking down, you idiot! warned the little voice in my head, and I pulled myself back from the edge of the basket, away from the dizzying view.

The view ahead was better. Less than a mile away,

through a gap between two skyscrapers, was an enticing glimpse of blue water. Sydney Harbor. But were we going to reach it? The wind was pushing us in the right direction, but the air in the balloon was cooling, and we were losing altitude fast.

I took another look down. It wasn't a reassuring sight. Even if I could steer the balloon, there was nowhere to land. The tops of all the buildings bristled with chimneys and ventilators and aerials, and there were cables, phone lines and electricity wires strung like spider webs over the streets.

The harbor was our only hope. I did a rough guesstimate, comparing our speed and angle of descent against the distance to the water. It was too far. We weren't going to make it.

BOMBS AWAY

I saw an old movie once where they made a balloon go up by throwing out bags of sand. The bags were called ballast. In the olden days, before balloon-makers had figured out how to make burners that turned on and off, ballast was part of a balloon's standard equipment. But modern hot air balloons don't have ballast, they have big gas bottles instead.

The bottles looked heavy.

"Jordan, give me a hand," I said.

I had already undone the wide, Velcro straps holding the two big silver bottles to the side of the basket, but I couldn't undo the gas lines because they were screwed on too tight. I figured it didn't matter

– the weight of the gas bottles would tear them free. I hoped so, anyway. If I was wrong, our number was up.

Jordan and I positioned ourselves one on either side of the first bottle. My little brother looked pale and trembly and weak. He was supposed to be taking it easy until I got him to a hospital, but this was an emergency. If dogs had hands, I would have gotten Myrtle to help, too. The bottles were nearly as big as me, and probably twice as heavy.

"One, two, three, *heave!*" I said.

The gas bottle was heavy, all right. I lifted nearly all its weight, but without Jordan's help I wouldn't have gotten it all the way up to the edge of the basket. We balanced it there for a moment, then gave it a push.

"Bombs away!" I yelled, and both of us ducked. It was lucky we did. There was a loud *bang* as the gas bottle ripped the reinforced rubber hose out of its fitting beneath the burner and dragged it over the side. Liquid propane sprayed in all directions. It was freezing cold. It turned to ice crystals on our hair and hands and clothing. If we hadn't ducked, it might have blinded us.

We got rid of the second gas bottle in the same way, being very careful this time to shield our faces and eyes. When the icy spray cleared, I looked over the side, hoping the bottles didn't land on anyone. I didn't see where the first one hit, but the second bottle exploded spectacularly in the middle of Martin Place. Luckily there was nobody close enough to get hurt, but I saw people taking cover as far away as George Street.

"Why are we trying to bomb people?" Jordan asked.

"We're not. We're making the balloon lighter so it won't crash in the city," I explained, gauging our rate of descent against a big office building to our left.

It had worked. Without the gas bottles aboard, we were no longer falling as fast as before. But we were still losing altitude. The tops of the several buildings were higher than us now. They loomed on either side of us like glass and concrete cliffs. The balloon drifted silently through the narrow canyon between them. I could hear the traffic below. A bus engine rumbled, a motorcycle went speeding along a street, a car tooted. I heard sirens, too. Had someone called the emergency services? I hoped so. But until we reached the harbor there was nothing anyone could do to help us. I could see the water glinting between the two skyscrapers ahead. It was no more than three or four hundred yards away. But there were several smaller buildings we had to cross first. Were we high enough?

Then I remembered the small red fire extinguisher. Unclipping it from its harness, I tested the weight of it in my hand. Would it make any difference? Little did I know that my fate – along with that of both Jordan and Myrtle – depended on the decision I was about to make.

With a sudden whirring of wings, a flock of pigeons came flying out of nowhere. They swirled all around us. One nearly hit me in the head. Myrtle went totally nuts. Barking and slobbering, she leapt up at the birds as they whirled past on all sides. I had to drop the fire extinguisher and grab the crazy dog to stop her from jumping out after them.

"Dogs can't fly, you silly mutt!" I said, wrestling her back into the basket.

The curious pigeons were still circling us, their noisy wings stirring Myrtle into a frenzy of excitement. She howled and bayed and struggled. It took both Jordan and me to restrain her. I had her in a bearhug – and she felt nearly *as big* as a bear – while Jordan held her head and tried to talk sense into her. His voice sounded wheezy, with long gaps between the words as if he'd just run a hundred-yard dash. The spider venom was doing its deadly work. I hoped one of the sirens was an ambulance.

When Myrtle calmed down, I looked over the side of the basket again. We'd floated over the low buildings and were crossing the ferry wharves at Circular Quay. We were about five hundred feet high and drifting straight towards the Opera House. There wasn't room to land on the narrow stretch of water between the wharves and Bennelong Point. I picked up the fire extinguisher, just in case, and watched the huge white sails of the Opera House looming ahead of us. For a moment I considered trying to land the balloon on the concrete forecourt between the harbor-side restaurants and the back of the Opera House, but decided not to take the risk. It would be safer to land on water than on concrete, and the harbor was only two hundred yards ahead.

We drifted slowly over the Opera House. I had been in Sydney only two weeks, and the closest I'd come to the city's most famous building was when we'd driven across the Harbor Bridge in Dad's four-wheel drive. *If only he hadn't gotten his stupid job,* I thought resentfully. The twins and I hadn't wanted to leave Crocodile Bridge; it was where we'd grown up. Dad and Mum both had perfectly good jobs at the local school, all our friends were there, and our big brother Nathan lived only five minutes away (three minutes if you took the BMX trail). And there weren't any Sydney funnel-web spiders.

"Hey, Jordan," I said over my shoulder. "How are you feeling?"

He didn't answer.

"Jordie, we're nearly ..." I started to say, but the rest of it died in my throat.

My little brother lay in the bottom of the basket with his eyes closed, and his head slumped sideways at a weird angle. Myrtle stood over him, whimpering. I took a closer look at him, then I felt like whimpering, too.

Jordan's face was blue.

TIME OF DEATH, 7:05 A.M.

I don't know how long after you stop breathing and your heart stops beating that you're officially dead. On TV shows, it's when the head of surgery looks up at the clock on the operating room wall and says, "Time of death, 7:05 a.m."

I guess I was acting head of surgery in the basket of VH-JZY, but I wasn't ready to pronounce Jordan dead. He was my brother. If he couldn't breathe on his own, then I'd do it for him. I gave him CPR.

The wind blew us out over Sydney Harbor, but there wasn't time to worry about landing. The balloon would have to take care of itself while I took care of Jordan. Crouching over him in the cramped confines of the basket, I pumped his small, bony rib cage with the heels of my hands, pausing every five compressions to blow air into his lungs like they'd taught us to do in first aid at my old high school. Five compressions then breathe, five compressions then breathe. Myrtle stood over us whimpering softly, and I'd swear there were tears in her sad brown eyes as she watched me giving my little brother CPR. Five compressions then breathe, five compressions then breathe.

This is all my stupid fault! I thought. I should have dropped the two-way radio while the funnel-web was still on it. Instead, I'd tried to shake the spider off, and the spider had landed on Jordan. Then bitten him.

And now he was ...

No, I said to myself. He *wasn't* dead. He couldn't be dead. He wasn't *allowed* to be dead!

Five compressions then breathe, five compressions then breathe.

My face was wet with tears, and I was sobbing uncontrollably as I pumped Jordan's skinny chest. *He isn't dead, isn't dead, isn't dead, isn't dead*, went the little voice in my head. But who was I trying to kid?

He still wasn't moving. Still wasn't breathing. His little five-year-old's heart still wasn't beating.

I'd lost all track of time. I had no idea how long I'd been giving him CPR. I only knew it wasn't working. It wasn't bringing Jordan back to life. I had to face facts: My little brother was ...

Thump!

WHAT I SAW

I should have been expecting it. The balloon had been losing altitude ever since its near-collision with the jumbo jet. But because of Jordan, I'd lost touch with reality. I'd forgotten I was in a balloon flying out of control across Sydney Harbor. I'd forgotten we were going to crash-land.

It didn't seem real when it happened. There must have been a lot of noise, but my ears didn't pass on the message to my shock-numbed brain. There must have been pain, too (I've got a black eye to prove it), but at the time I felt nothing. It was as if I was someone else, some*where* else, watching it on TV with the sound turned down.

Here's what I saw: flashes of rocks and trees and sky; a tall concrete wall bumping underneath the tipped-over basket; sparks from the burners as they scraped over steel and concrete; Jordan, Myrtle and me flopping around like rag dolls; silver wires twisting and twirling all around us; the shredded balloon billowing overhead; a frenzy of whirling trees and thrashing leaves and whipping branches …

Then the fire extinguisher came bouncing up straight at my face and – *whack!* – the TV went off.

LARGEST MEAT-EATER ON FOUR LEGS

Oooooooow! My head throbbed. It felt like a horse had kicked me. Now it was breathing on my face. I opened my eyes. And was greeted by the sight of Myrtle's wet black nose and big, slobbery muzzle about two inches away.

"Get off, you mutt," I groaned, pushing her aside.

I was lying on my back in the bottom of the basket. There was a tangle of wires and cables above me, and the twisted remains of the burners. But no balloon.

No balloon!

Looking up out of the basket, all I could see was a sheer concrete wall and a patch of white cloudy sky.

The balloon had landed. Well, it had *crash*-landed, but at least it was safely on the ground. And I was still alive.

But Jordan wasn't. My eyes filled with tears when I remembered what happened just before the crash. Slowly, I sat up. My little brother lay beside me in a sprawl of skinny arms and legs. He looked really small in my oversized T-shirt. Myrtle was licking his face.

"Stop that!" I said crossly, dragging her aside.

Jordan's small bluish-white face looked almost peaceful. His eyes were half-open. I reached over to close them, but just as I did, one of his eyelids twitched. I jerked my hand back as if I'd seen a ghost.

"Jordan?" I whispered, crouching over him.

He didn't move. His eyes seemed to stare right through me. At that moment, the sun broke through the clouds. It was too low in the sky to shine into the basket, but a single golden ray reflected down off the twisted stainless steel burners, directly into Jordan's right eye. The pupil contracted to a tiny dot.

My heart nearly jumped clean up my throat. Was he alive? Had the CPR worked?

"Jordan, can you hear me?" I whispered.

There was no reaction. His eyes continued to stare

straight through me. I put my ear close to his mouth. I thought I could hear a faint, wheezy sound like a mouse breathing, but it was hard to be sure with Myrtle panting like a steam train in my other ear. I grabbed one of Jordan's wrists and found the pulse point. Yes! It was faint and thready, but there was definitely a pulse.

Jordan was alive!

I wanted to hug him and shout for joy, but I knew it was too soon to celebrate. He was unconscious. He'd been bitten by a funnel-web. His heart had already stopped once, and it might stop again at any moment. I had to get help – which shouldn't have been a problem now that the balloon had landed. After all, we were in Sydney.

But nothing could have prepared me for what I saw when I scrambled to my feet and looked over the side of the basket.

Shishkebab!

Looking back at me was the biggest head I'd ever seen. That's not quite true – I'd seen bigger heads on elephants and whales and Clydesdale horses, and maybe even on a bull crocodile I tangled with once – but when you come face-to-face with a Kodiak bear, it's hard to put things in perspective.

We had crashed in the zoo! The wind must have freshened when we'd drifted across the harbor and pushed the balloon all the way to Taronga Park on the other shore. It was bad luck that we'd landed in the bear pit, rather than in with the giraffes or the giant tortoises, or any other of the zoo's many harmless inhabitants. But our luck hadn't run out entirely. The balloon's support wires had snagged on the fifty-foot-high wall surrounding the pit, leaving us dangling just out of the bear's reach.

Along with the polar bear, the Kodiak bear is the world's largest meat-eater on four legs. And this one was standing on two legs, so its head was really close – only a foot and a half below the basket. It seemed to be frowning, as if it didn't quite know what to make of us. It probably saw hundreds of people every day – but not up close. Not inside its enclosure. The bear's broad, flat-tipped nose quivered and made a loud, snuffling noise as it checked out our scent. Myrtle jumped up against the side of the basket to see what was going on. One look at the huge bear was enough. She reeled back in fright and cowered on the floor next to Jordan, whimpering like a scared puppy. We were trapped.

"*Help!*" I yelled, at the top of my voice. "*Help! Can anyone hear me?*"

Lots of animals heard me – the chimpanzees started screeching, an elephant trumpeted, and a big cat growled somewhere close by – but no people. It was only ten past seven in the morning. The zookeepers mustn't be at work yet.

My shouting brought a second bear from a cave-like opening in the wall of the pit. It was even bigger than the first bear. When it stood up on its hind legs and stretched up with its paws, it could just touch the basket. Its massive claws tore at the wooden skids beneath the creaking cane floor, sending wood splinters flying, and rocking us back and forth. The thin, steel wires supporting us creaked and twanged.

There wasn't much holding us up. The wires disappeared over the top of the wall, where part of the deflated balloon dangled into the pit like a collapsed circus tent. If the wires snapped or tore free, we would crash to the ground. And the bears would have us for breakfast.

I ducked down to check on Jordan. It took a while to find a pulse. He was still alive, but only just. He needed antivenin. The zookeepers would probably start arriving some time in the next hour. It was too long to wait. In an hour the funnel-web's venom would have already done its deadly work.

Something clicked in my brain. It put two words together: antivenin and zoo. That was it! They had snakes at the zoo, so it stood to reason there would be a supply of antivenin in case one of the keepers got bitten. And this was the *Sydney* zoo – it was more than likely they'd have Sydney funnel-webs on display. So ...

I put Jordan into the recovery position. "Take care of him, Myrtle," I said.

Trying not to look down at the bears just below me, I scrambled up onto the edge of the basket and steadied myself against the twisted burner assembly. The wall was fifty feet high and absolutely sheer. There were no handholds. I couldn't climb the wires; they would cut my hands to shreds. But I might be able to scale the wall using the vent rope. It dangled against the concrete on the other side of the basket. Carefully, I worked my way around its padded edge. Below me, one of the bears made a loud, yawny growl. It sounded like Chewbacca in the *Star Wars* movies. I wished I was in a movie, and this was just a stunt. Then there'd be safety nets to catch me if I fell, not Kodiak bears.

Just as I reached for the rope, the bigger bear gave the basket another whack. I lost my balance, grabbing for the rope as I fell. My hands closed around it, but instead of taking my weight, the rope seemed to come loose from its moorings. I slid down the wall, totally helpless. All I could do was hold on and hope for the best. My knuckles, elbows and knees scraped against the concrete. Suddenly, there was a twang, and the rope snapped taut. I found myself dangling halfway down the basket. On the outside.

Uh-oh!

Everything seemed to happen in a blur. Something bumped against my right leg. I felt warm breath on my ankle. Out of the corner of my eye, I glimpsed a huge brown and pink shape. The pink was the inside of the bear's wide-open mouth. I corkscrewed my body and pulled my legs up. *Clunk!* The huge jaws missed me by inches. But now the second bear got into the action. Coming from the other direction, it took a wild swing at me. *Swoosh!* Its big black claws carved through the air like daggers.

Desperately, I twisted away. My left foot bumped into the other bear. It opened its mouth to bite me, but I kicked it in the nose. Roaring like Chewbacca, it lost its balance and fell backwards against the wall. I wasn't sure where the other bear was, but I didn't wait to find out. Powered by adrenalin, I pulled my body up out of the bears' reach, then dragged myself, hand over hand, all the way to the top of the rope.

The last six feet were the hardest. I had to clamber over a huge bundle of red, blue and yellow nylon: the remains of the balloon. When we'd crashed, one of the basket's support wires had snagged on an iron spike at the top of the wall, and the balloon had collapsed over it. The rope disappeared under the nylon, so I had to grab big handfuls of the slippery fabric to pull myself up. It was very hard work, but finally I made it. On my hands and knees, I crawled up onto the wide, flat platform at the top of the wall. And stopped dead.

Shishkebab!

Ten feet away crouched a big golden-maned lion.

BRING IT ON, SIMBA

It felt like a dream. A very bad one. Seeing the bears for the first time had seemed freaky enough – until I'd realized we were at the zoo. But a *lion*? Okay, I know I was still at the zoo. But I wasn't in an enclosure, and neither was the lion. Did they let lions run loose at Taronga Zoo? Not likely.

I rose slowly to my feet.

The lion's big golden eyes followed me. He growled. I almost took a step backwards, then remembered where I was. It was a long fall back into the bear pit. Instinctively, I glanced over my shoulder. *Ohmygosh*, I was so high! I could see the Opera House in the distance, and the city and the Harbor Bridge. A tiny green ferry inched across the water like a child's toy. I wished I was on it. Anywhere but here.

There was no escape. The lion and I were on top of a fifty-foot-high wall separating the bear pit from the enclosure next to it. The wall was flat-topped and about six feet wide. I couldn't see what lived next door to the bears, but it didn't take a genius to figure it out: lions. A skinny date palm growing inside the enclosure had been uprooted. It leaned against the wall at a forty-five-degree angle. The basket must have knocked the palm down as we flew across the lions' pit, and the lion had climbed up its trunk.

Nice kitty, I tried to say, but my mouth was dry with fear, and all that came out was a rasping sound.

The lion put his ears back, and the tip of his tail started to twitch. *Gulp!* When Tibbles our cat was a kitten, that's exactly what she used to do when she was about to spring on a toy mouse.

Very slowly, I started backing away from the lion along the top of the wall. He licked his chops. I was cornered, and we both knew it. I couldn't jump off the wall – I'd land in the bear pit on one side, or the lions' den on the other. Even in the unlikely event that the fall didn't kill me, I would still wind up on someone's breakfast menu.

Walking backwards, I reached the tangled fabric of the deflated balloon. I stepped onto it and – hooley dooley! – the two layers of slippery nylon went in two directions, pitching me onto my backside. *Thump!*

I must have looked completely helpless because the lion didn't even bother charging. He simply rose from his crouch and came padding confidently towards me.

"*Stop!*" I yelled, at the top of my voice.

That was something I'd learned at karate: If you're being attacked, a loud shout will sometimes surprise your opponent and cause them to hesitate. In that split second of indecision, they are vulnerable to a counterattack.

It worked. The lion checked his stride.

I had no intention of making a counterattack – the odds were stacked a million to one in the lion's favor. But I had a plan that might even things up a bit.

In the three or four seconds I gained when the lion hesitated, I wriggled away from him across the slippery nylon on the seat of my jeans. When I reached the other side, I knelt on the concrete facing the giant cat and gripped the edge of the nylon firmly in both hands. Nervously I wet my lips.

"Bring it on, Simba," I murmured.

THE REAL TRICK

The lion snarled and came stalking towards me. He looked wary now. He knew I was up to something, but he wasn't sure exactly what.

As soon as the lion stepped onto the nylon, he found out.

"Yaaaaah!" I yelled.

This time the shout didn't work. The lion wasn't going to fall for the same trick twice. But he wasn't expecting my other trick, the *real* trick.

Even as I was shouting, I jumped to my feet. Raising the edge of the balloon in front of me, I rushed at the lion. It was the last thing the lion expected. Taken by surprise, he tried to leap over the approaching wall of billowing fabric, but his paws skidded on the slippery nylon, and he blundered headfirst into it instead. I spun out of the way, holding the raised section of the balloon at arms' length like a bullfighter's cape as the lion went sliding underneath. Turning as the lion went past, I twirled the fabric down over his haunches and tail, enclosing him in a twist of red, blue and yellow nylon.

The lion did the rest. Finding himself wrapped up in the balloon, he went completely psycho. He struggled and twisted and rolled over and over and over, roaring with rage and slashing blindly at the flimsy sheath that held him prisoner. The balloon fabric was light, but it was made of special high-tenacity, non-rip nylon. Even the lion's razor-sharp claws had difficulty tearing it. The more he struggled, the more entangled he became.

I stood well clear, keeping one eye on the bucking, twisting shape of the lion, and the other on the edge of the wall. I didn't want him to fall in with the bears – Jordan was down there. When at last the enraged animal seemed to be tiring, I took a handful of loose nylon and tried dragging the bundle away from the bears' side of the wall. But a fully grown male lion weighs nearly four hundred and fifty pounds; I couldn't budge him. The lion felt me straining on his woven prison and made a wild slash at me. One of his razor-sharp claws punched a hole through the nylon, ripping my jeans open all the way from the knee to the ankle. I jumped backwards, slipped, and nearly fell into the lions' pit, just saving myself by grabbing one of the big, spiky fronds of the palm tree.

My feet dangled in midair. When I looked down, I saw three lionesses fifty feet below, waiting for me to fall. It was all the incentive I needed to swing myself back up onto the edge of the wall. Palm fronds jiggled and rustled all around me. The lion was only three feet away. He couldn't see me, but he heard my struggles. With a thunderous roar, he lurched blindly in my direction, crashing into my shoulder and trying to bite me through the nylon. Luckily, his jaws closed around one of the palm fronds, not my arm. While he chewed on the crackling foliage, I managed to scramble past him to safety. But I was only safe as long as the lion remained tangled in the folds of the balloon. Already there were several big rips. My inclination was to turn and run, but I knew what I had to do.

The lion's struggles had taken him right to the edge of the wall. Part of him hung over the pit below. Bending down, I gathered up two big handfuls of nylon and lifted.

Slowly, like a pea being shelled from its pod, the big, squirming bulge slid further and further over the edge of the wall. Then, with a deep growl of anger, the lion rolled down the steep, sloping trunk of the palm tree and landed on his feet next to the three lionesses.

Wicked! Not only had I outsmarted the lion, I'd put him back in his enclosure. But there wasn't time to savor my narrow escape; I had to get help for Jordan.

I ran to the end of the wall and skidded to a halt. It was a dead end. I was at the front of the bears' and lions' enclosures, faced with a sheer drop of fifty feet to the viewing area, where visitors could watch the animals through long, reinforced windows with iron spikes along the top. There was no way down. I would have to go back the way I'd come and look for an escape route at the rear of the enclosures. I turned around to retrace my steps. And froze.

The lion was halfway back up the palm tree.

WHUFF!

The uprooted palm leaned against the wall about sixty-five feet away. I forced myself to run back towards it. Back towards the lion. He was nearly at the top. My feet didn't want to move, but I had to get past, or I'd be trapped at the end of the wall. With nowhere to go except down. Fifty feet was too far to jump.

The lion had only about six feet to go, but he was having trouble keeping his balance. Lions aren't good tree climbers like leopards, and the trunk became quite skinny towards the top. There was the added problem of the palm fronds, which formed a wide, prickly barrier ahead of him. He roared when he saw me coming and wobbled up another foot or so. I reached the tangled folds of the balloon and had to slow down – I couldn't risk falling over again. I came level with the lion. His massive head looked bigger than a Kodiak bear's through the trembling palm fronds. He roared again, and the air seemed to shake. I was almost past him when the grim reality of my situation hit me. No way was I going to escape. The lion would crash through the palm fronds in a matter of moments. Then he'd come after me. Lions are fast. Even if there was a way down over the back of the enclosures, he would catch me long before I got to safety.

I was past the lion now, but I stopped and went back. It felt like a stupid thing to do – and it would be the *last* thing I did if it didn't work – but it was my only chance. I grabbed two of the big green fronds that stuck up out of his enclosure. The lion was so close I could have touched him. He roared once more, and I could smell his stale, meaty breath. When I started pulling the fronds sideways, the trunk slid sideways too, with the lion clinging to it. He hissed like an oversized domestic cat and made a desperate lunge for the top of the wall. His claws left a series of deep, parallel tracks in the concrete as I heaved the uprooted palm past its point of balance. With a crackle of fronds, it began to slide down the inside wall of the pit. For a moment, the lion and I were eye to eye. Then, with a frustrated yowl, both he and the palm tree disappeared from view and went crashing back into the lions' enclosure where they belonged.

There wasn't a moment to lose. While I'd been battling the lion, Jordan was fighting a battle of his own – with the deadly spider's venom. At least, I hoped he was still fighting it ...

I ran to the rear of the enclosure with my fingers crossed. *Please, please, please, let there be a way down!* I prayed. I looked over the edge. Yes! Attached to the wall six feet below me was a small building. It looked like a pretend African hut, with a semicircular roof thatched with straw and sticks. I lowered myself gingerly onto the thatch. It crunched under my feet, but supported my weight. Carefully, I scrambled down to the edge. It was ten feet to the dusty ground, and there was nothing to hold onto to make the drop any easier. I looked around. At the opposite side of the hut was a large peppercorn tree that drooped its thick green foliage onto the roof. I climbed down through the branches and dropped the last foot and a half to the ground. Made it!

The hut didn't have walls, it was just a thatched roof held up by stout wooden poles like a picnic shelter. I didn't want shelter; I wanted to find a building with *First Aid* on the door – somewhere with a medicine cabinet containing antivenin. I looked around for other buildings, or a sign with directions. It seemed a strange place to have a picnic shelter – very dusty and nothing to look at except a six-foot-high concrete wall with gaps in it every ten or twelve paces. There were iron bars in the gaps, like sections of a cage. I wondered what was on the other side. *It must be a big animal*, I thought, because the bars were very thick.

Whuff!

I jumped. The noise came from behind me – from the shelter. I turned around.

Shishkebab!

I hadn't noticed the animal before because it had been standing quietly in the shadows at the back of the shelter, and it was gray like the concrete wall behind it. But when it came trotting out into the light, I realized why the iron bars were so thick. It was a rhino.

And I was *inside* its enclosure!

HISSSSSSSSS!

In books they say that rhinos don't have very good eyesight. If ever you're chased by one, you are supposed to run in a zigzag so the rhino won't be able to see you properly and will charge straight past. I'll bet the person who wrote that has never been chased by a rhino. I have. You go in a straight line – you can't help it.

I ran straight towards the nearest gap in the wall. There were bars in the gap, but I wasn't thinking about that. I was thinking only about what was behind me. Rhinos are big. An adult male can weigh up to three tons. This was a female, she probably weighed about two tons, but she looked as big as a house. And she was fast – much faster than me. I could hear her getting closer with every stride. The ground shook. *Whuff, whuff, whuff,* went her breath just behind me, so close I felt it on the naked skin of my back. My arms pumped, my legs were a blur, and the ripped right leg of my jeans flapped wildly around my shins like a tattered blue flag.

I threw myself at the bars and went straight up them.

Clanggggg!

The rhino's horn smacked into the iron barrier at about twenty-five miles per hour. Shock waves ran up and down the bars, loosening a hundred tiny chips of concrete that exploded into the air all around me. I reached the top and hurled myself over, landing heavily on the gravel path on the other side. My heart was beating at about two hundred beats per minute, and my chest was heaving. I had skinned both hands when I'd landed, but I felt no pain. I'd escaped. I was outside the rhino's enclosure, and she was inside. Two of the bars were slightly bent. The rhino snorted at me through the gap and shook her big, ugly head as if to say, *you're lucky!*

I didn't feel lucky as I limped away. *But Jordan was*

even unluckier than me, I reminded myself, increasing my pace. I had no idea where I was going. Everything hinged on there being a supply of funnel-web antivenin at the zoo.

But even if there was some here, where would they keep it?

I passed the giraffes, the mountain sheep, an aviary full of noisy yellow parrots, then I reached an intersection. Paths led off in three directions, with signposts directing the way to various exhibits. None said first aid, but there was one that caught my eye. It had three symbols on it.

I stared at the middle one. *Wouldn't it make sense,* I thought, *to keep antivenin somewhere close to where it might be needed?*

Then my feet were running, taking me in the direction the sign pointed.

I reached a squat, concrete-and-brick building surrounded by gardens and trees. *Serpentaria,* said a large, wooden sign, along with the three symbols.

An arrow pointed to the entrance. I ran to the door, but it was locked. I gave it a thump with my shoulder. It was solid. Frustrated, I looked at my watch. 7:22. It might be another thirty or forty minutes before anyone arrived, and that would be too late for Jordan.

I ran around the side of the building, searching for another way in. There was a tiny, rectangular opening in the bricks, like a miniature window except it didn't have glass. I crossed a cactus garden to look in. Through the hole was a small courtyard filled with ferns, shiny-leafed bushes and other exotic plants. It was open to the sky – I could climb in.

The wall was ten feet high, but I used the hole to hoist myself up. I scrambled over the top and lowered myself into the courtyard. I had to drop the final eight inches. My right foot landed on a big gray log, which rolled sideways and sent me crashing backwards onto the hard ground.

For a couple of seconds I lay on my back. Nothing felt broken, but I was a bit dazed. I'd landed hard, and my head was throbbing from the knock I'd received earlier when the balloon crashed. How long ago was that? Probably ten or fifteen minutes. It seemed more like ten *hours*, so much had happened since.

Hissssssssss!

What was that?

Slowly, I turned my head.

I wasn't in a courtyard; I was in a kind of pit. It was much smaller than the bear pit and filled with ferns, bushes and rocks. One of the rocks was made of concrete and had a low cave underneath it. The cave was less than six feet from where I lay. And waddling out of the cave was a … was a …

(I blinked in disbelief)

… dinosaur!

DRAGON FOOD

At least it *looked* like a dinosaur. The Komodo dragon is the world's largest lizard. They're also the most dangerous. Scientists have found over fifty different types of disease-ridden bacteria living in their deadly, serrated teeth. One bite from a Komodo dragon, and its victim will die of blood poisoning within forty-eight hours.

This one had me cornered. I lay squashed against the bricks, too scared to move a muscle, as the giant reptile sized me up. It was bigger than me, about ten feet long, with massive, body-builder's shoulders, legs as thick as a man's thighs and claws like meat hooks. But its head was the worst part. Imagine a goanna crossed with a crocodile, give it warty, gray skin, a long, yellow forked tongue and breath so foul you want to throw up. That's what confronted me as I cowered against the wall, and the hideous creature was only three feet away.

In the wild, Komodo dragons eat deer, pigs, water buffalo, wild horses, birds, snakes, fish, crabs, snails and insects – just about anything, in fact. At the zoo they only get dead rats. This Komodo dragon looked ready for a change of diet. It flicked its tongue at me, testing the air for my scent. I must have smelled okay because it puffed out its long, warty throat like an inner tube inflating, opened its putrid mouth and lunged at me.

I was cornered, I had nowhere to go. *And* I was lying down. All I could do was fend it off with my feet. Or try to. The giant lizard was too big and strong. It pushed past my sneakers and bit savagely at my right calf. *Snap!* The terrible jaws narrowly missed my leg, closing instead on the trailing edge of my torn jeans. The dragon began shaking its head from side to side, like a dog playing tug-of-war games with a stick or a rope. But this wasn't a stick or a rope, it was my leg. And the dragon wasn't playing games. If a single one of those germ-infected teeth so much as nicked my skin, there was a better-than-even chance I would die of blood-poisoning, regardless of whether or not I got to the hospital and was given antibiotics. And if the dragon got its jaws around my leg, I wouldn't even get to the hospital – they'd take me (or what remained of me) straight to the morgue.

They'd take Jordan there, too.

I desperately pulled the other way. But the huge lizard had a body weight advantage of roughly three to one. It started dragging me on my backside towards the cave. Once it got me into its lair, my fate was sealed – I'd be dragon food.

I grabbed hold of a passing bush, but it tore out by the roots. I kicked at the dragon with my free foot, I clawed at the ground. Nothing worked. The dragon was unstoppable. It started pulling me under the rock. First the dragon disappeared, then my feet, then my shins.

I was going to die!

Think, Sam! said the little voice in my head. Actually, it was my big brother Nathan's voice – he's good at getting out of tight situations. *Use your head, Sam!* it said.

I did use my head. The dragon had a hold of my jeans, not my leg. With fumbly fingers, I got the button undone, then I loosened the zipper and wriggled my hips out of my jeans. For a few panicky moments my left sneaker became caught in the denim, then there was a loud, ripping sound, and suddenly I was free.

I scrabbled away from the dragon's lair and leapt to my feet. The giant lizard came wriggling out after me. It still had my jeans in its mouth. I danced away from it, nearly tripping in some ferns, and jumped over a log. The dragon took the long way around. It gave me about two seconds to search for a way to escape. The pit was about thirteen feet wide. There was a low concrete wall on the other side with a Plexiglas window on top for visitors to look through. The top of the Plexiglas was about six feet high. As the dragon came crashing through the bushes towards me, I took a running jump and vaulted over the concrete-and-Plexiglas barrier. I landed without hurting myself. There was a bit of gravel-rash on my palms from using them as brakes when the Komodo dragon had tried to drag me into its lair, but not a scratch on my legs or ankles. Once again, I'd been lucky.

But I'd lost my jeans. Wearing only boxer shorts and sneakers, I surveyed my surroundings. I was inside the Serpentaria, on a brick-paved path that wound its way through a long, walled yard past a series of pits similar to the Komodo dragon's. There was a building at the end, and its door was open. I hurried towards it, hoping to find funnel-web spiders. Because if they had funnel-web spiders, they might have a supply of antivenin.

They have to have it! I thought, fighting back tears. Otherwise Jordan was going to die.

FURRY MOUNTAINS

There was just about every type of snake imaginable, as well as lizards, tortoises, frogs, scorpions and giant tarantulas. Each species was housed in its own glass-fronted display, set into the walls on both sides like miniature shop windows in a mall. I rushed up and down, reading the labels on the glass with an increasing sense of panic. At last, two windows from the end, was a label that said, *Sydney Funnel-web Spider.*

I didn't think I would ever be pleased to see a funnel-web, but it felt like winning the lottery.

Okay, I thought, *where do they keep the antivenin?*

I quickly retraced my steps. Halfway along one

row of exhibits was a door set into a recess between two windows. There must be a room at the back. A sign said, *Staff Only*. Not surprisingly, the door was locked. I pushed with my shoulder, but it wouldn't budge. I tried kicking it. No good. The door was solid. I looked at my watch. 7:28. I couldn't wait for someone to arrive. Jordan's life hung in the balance. I had to break in. But how?

Something didn't make sense. The glass at the front of each exhibit was set firmly into the wall – it couldn't open – so how did the keepers feed the creatures and clean their cages? Once I thought about it, the answer was obvious: from the back. From the room where I wanted to go!

Sure enough, when I looked in through the nearest window (*Horned Rattlesnake,* said the label) I saw a hinged door on the other side. I nervously moved up and down the row of windows, looking for one that didn't have something dangerous or majorly creepy on the other side of the glass. They were nearly all snakes. No way was I going to crawl through one of their cages! Finally, I came to a display containing lots of tiny blue frogs. *Poison Arrow Frogs*, the label said. I knew their poison was deadly, but they secreted it from their skin – I'd have to touch one and then lick my hand for it to affect me (and there was no way I was going to do that!). Besides, they were really small, not much bigger than my thumbnail. Compared to the snakes and scorpions and spiders, they looked harmless. Little did I know that there was enough poison in just one of those tiny blue frogs to kill a hundred humans!

It would have stopped me from doing what I was about to do.

The glass looked thick. I remembered passing a cactus in an earthenware flowerpot just outside the entrance to the building. I ran to get it.

"Take cover, frogs," I muttered, and hurled the pot at the window.

Smash! Glass, dirt, bits of flowerpot, and cactus flew everywhere. Using a piece of broken earthenware, I chipped away the jagged teeth of glass around the window's gaping frame. Then I pulled out some of the sticks and vines and leafy branches inside the display. A tiny blue frog jumped over my shoulder, but I ignored it. Careful not to put my hands on any broken glass or bits of cactus, I climbed into the poison arrow frogs' cage. It was cramped.

I had to bend my back and duck my head. My ear brushed against a sticky vine, and another frog went crawling down the wall like a blue spider. I was glad they didn't bite. The back of the display creaked when I applied pressure. I gave it a thump, and a small, rectangular panel swung open. Sweet! Behind the display was a long, narrow room. I wormed through the opening and dropped to the floor.

It looked like a laboratory. There were benches cluttered with cages and jars and scientific equipment, and shelves and charts lining the walls. A first-aid sign on a white cabinet drew me like a magnet. Among the surgical dressings, bandages, lotions and eyewashes inside, I found some syringes wrapped in cellophane. But no antivenin. I looked desperately around the room. A syringe was a good start, now I needed something to put in it. Where would they keep the antivenin? My eyes were drawn to a small fridge at the far end of the room. I hadn't taken any notice of it at first, but now I remembered that some medicines are kept under refrigeration. I hurried across to it. In a plastic tray on one of the shelves were about two dozen small white boxes with medical labels on them. The first one I picked up said,

Common Brown Snake, Antivenin.

I rummaged through the tray, in such a hurry that several little boxes clattered to the floor around my feet. *Coral Snake, Horned Rattlesnake, Gaboon Viper, Mulga Snake, King Cobra, Red-back Spider, Scorpion.* There seemed to be antivenin for every venomous creature on earth – except the one I wanted.

Then, right at the bottom, there it was: *Sydney Funnel-web, Antivenin.* Bingo!

I opened the box and carefully took out the tiny glass ampoule. It resembled a miniature bowling pin and was filled with clear liquid. Jordan's life depended on those few tiny drops. I slipped the precious ampoule back into its box for safety and ran to get one of the syringes.

All the door locks opened from the inside. I was out of the Serpentaria in fifteen seconds, running flat out back the way I'd come.

I charged around a corner and nearly ran into a small white van coming the other way. It skidded to a halt, and the driver's door swung open.

"Stop right there!" said a woman in a zookeeper's uniform, stepping out onto the road in front of me.

I tried to swerve around her, but she grabbed my

arm. She had a very strong grip. We swung in a circle.

"Let go!" I cried. "I've got to get back to my brother."

"You're not going anywhere," she puffed, red-faced from the effort of holding on. "What's that in your hand? What have you been up to?"

I must have looked pretty dodgy, wearing only boxer shorts and sneakers, and holding a syringe in my hand. "It's not what you think," I said desperately. "My brother's been bitten by a funnel-web. Our balloon crashed in the bear pit."

Her eyes widened, and she released my arm. "What bears?"

"The Kodiaks," I said, and raced off down the path.

"Hey, wait!" she cried. "Come back! Show me where your brother is!"

No way was I going back. Once she saw where Jordan was, the zookeeper wouldn't let me anywhere near him. They would have to lock the bears up, then get a rescue crew with ladders and a stretcher. It would take ages, and Jordan didn't *have* ages.

"Call an ambulance!" I yelled, over my shoulder. And kept running. I had to get to Jordan.

The rhino was down at the far end of the enclosure with its back to me. It didn't see me squeeze between the bent iron bars and rush across to the peppercorn tree. Climbing it was difficult with the syringe and antivenin in one hand, but my brother's life was at stake, and it only took a few seconds to scramble onto the thatched roof of the rhino's shelter. Moments later I dragged myself up onto the wide, concrete parapet at the rear of the bear pit. The big golden-maned lion looked up at me as I raced along the top of the wall. I reached the balloon and peered cautiously over the edge. Both bears were down near the viewing area at the front of the enclosure. They had seen me, but they weren't the problem. Climbing down to the basket wasn't going to be easy. It dangled thirty or forty feet below me. I could see Myrtle curled up on the floor and Jordan lying next to her. He hadn't moved since I last saw him. I hoped with all my heart that I wasn't too late.

I needed two hands to climb down to the basket, but I had the syringe and the antivenin and no pockets to put them in. The only solution was to stuff them into the top of my sneakers. I found the balloon's vent rope in the tangle of nylon, gripped it firmly in both hands and took a deep breath. It made me dizzy to look down, so I descended backwards, walking slowly down the side of the pit like a geriatric abseiler, and keeping my eyes focused on the gray concrete directly in front of me.

Something moved in my hair. At first I thought a fly had landed on me. Then it crawled onto my ear. It was much too heavy to be a fly. I could feel its feet clinging to my skin.

Funnel-web spider! shrieked the little voice in my head.

It wasn't a logical thought. Why would there be a funnel-web spider on me? Where would it have come from? But I was so stressed I wasn't thinking clearly, and in my brain there was an image of the funnel-web landing on Jordan's head.

Without considering my precarious situation, I reached up to brush it away. Big mistake. I needed two hands to support my weight. As soon as I let go with one, the rope began to slide through the sweaty palm of the other.

The next moment, I was falling.

Luckily, I didn't have far to fall. The balloon's burner-assembly was only three or four feet below me. I hit it with a jarring clang and landed spread-eagled across the padded rim of the basket.

Then, from high above me, there came a loud *twang!*

Ever since we'd crashed, the basket had been supported by a single steel wire wrapped around the iron spike at the top of the wall. The jolt when I landed on the basket's rim caused the cable to snap. With nothing to hold it up, the basket slid the rest of the way down the wall and hit the ground with a bump, throwing me clear.

For a few moments I didn't move. I was lying on my stomach in soft sand. I knew where I was – in the bear pit! – but my brain felt fuzzy. Beside me, only a few inches from my nose, was a blurred, blue, vaguely spider-like shape. I focused my eyes on it. A poison arrow frog. That's what had crawled onto my ear. It must have gotten tangled in my hair when I climbed through its cage back in the Serpentaria. Now it was dead. I had squashed it when I landed.

I heard whimpering and looked up. The basket was six feet away. Myrtle had her paws on the edge. She was peering over my head, her ears back, and her eyes big with fear. I turned to see what she was looking at.

Holy guacamole!

Lumbering towards me at about thirty miles per hour were two brown furry mountains!

SURPRISE BEATS SIZE

The sight of the charging bears shook me out of my daze. In two seconds I was upright, vaulting into the basket. I bowled Myrtle over and nearly landed on Jordan. My right foot came down heavily on the fire extinguisher. It rolled sideways, pulling a tendon in my ankle. But I hardly felt it. Was Jordan still alive? There wasn't time to check. There wasn't time to give him antivenin.

Crouched next to Myrtle over Jordan's small lifeless form in the bottom of the basket, I listened to the bears pounding towards us. The ground shook. At roughly a thousand pounds apiece, their combined weight was about equal to a small car. I hoped their brakes were just as good. At the very last moment, when I judged they were less than fifteen feet away, I jumped up in the basket like a jack-in-the-box.

Surprise beats size, my karate instructor once told me. The last thing the bears expected was to be attacked by a puny, half-naked human who (they thought) was about to become their breakfast. And they'd probably never been sprayed by a fire extinguisher before.

Both animals skidded to a halt only a foot or two from the basket. I directed the hissing jet of foam back and forth in their faces. It was too much for the smaller bear. Shaking its huge, wet head, it turned tail and went lumbering away. The larger bear bellowed and rose up on its hind legs, towering over the basket. It was huge! It snapped and bit at the spray and swatted the air with its massive forepaws. I raised the fire extinguisher as high as I could and gave the animal a blast right in the eyes. Momentarily blinded, the thousand-pound monster shuffled backwards, lost its footing and fell on its backside.

The fire extinguisher made a fizzing noise, and the jet of spray diminished to a dribble of gray, bubbly water, then stopped altogether. I shook it, but nothing happened. It was empty. The bear watched me with its small, piggy eyes. Sitting on the ground only ten feet from the basket, it waggled its wet, shaggy head from side to side and sneezed a couple of times. I pointed the fire extinguisher at it (the bear didn't know it was empty), took a deep breath and made a loud hissing sound.

It worked! The bear flinched and turned its head away. Rolling to its feet, it lumbered off to join its companion, which had retreated to a cave-like recess in the far wall of the bear pit.

I knelt down to check on Jordan. He was alive, but still unconscious. He looked worse than before. His lips were blue, and his eyelids twitched. He was hanging on to life by a thread. I'd reached him in the nick of time. Pulling the syringe from my right sneaker, I ripped the wrapping off it. Then I dug down into my left sneaker for the antivenin. All I found was the tiny cardboard box. Squashed flat and empty. The ampoule had fallen out!

I frantically rummaged around on the floor of the basket (I even looked under Jordan), but the antivenin wasn't there. The ampoule must have slipped out of its box while I was climbing down the rope. I stood up and looked over the side, but it was hopeless – the ampoule was tiny; it could be anywhere. Even under the basket. A wave of despair settled over me. I could hardly believe it – after everything I'd been through, after all the crazy risks I'd taken to get the antivenin, I'd gone and *lost* it!

Jordan was going to die.

I blinked and leaned over the side of the basket. Something had caught my eye. A glint of silver in the sand. It was exactly where I'd ended up when the basket crashed to the floor of the pit. It looked like glass. The ampoule! I couldn't see whether or not it was broken because it was partially buried in the sand. *Please don't be broken*, I prayed, and began climbing out of the basket.

Then stopped.

One of the bears was coming back. The bigger one. The meaner one. It looked *really* mean now. It stalked slowly towards the basket with its teeth bared, and its beady black eyes fixed on me. I knew immediately what was going to happen. As soon as I left the basket, it would charge.

But I had to leave the basket to get the antivenin.

There wasn't a moment to lose. The bear was

ninety feet away and closing. I pushed Myrtle aside and picked up the empty fire extinguisher, then swung my legs over the side and jumped to the ground. Pointing it at the bear, I took two steps towards the half-buried ampoule (and towards the bear).

"Hissssssssss!" I said.

This time the bear wasn't fooled. It charged.

Over short distances, Kodiak bears can run as fast as horses. It was a terrifying sight. But I didn't stop. I couldn't stop. I *had* to get the ampoule. Darting forward, I scooped it up. It wasn't broken. I started backing away from the huge, charging bear, but I was too late. It was nearly on top of me. In desperation, I flung the fire extinguisher. The bear snapped at it, teeth clanged on metal. I tripped and fell, twisting my body sideways. I hit the ground rolling. The bear's reflexes were lightning fast. It swerved and came after me. It was huge. It blocked out the sky.

My left hand closed around something cold and sticky in the sand.

When the bear opened its huge mouth to crush out my life, I flicked my fingers upwards. A tiny blue object flew straight into the bear's gaping pink maw.

If a human swallowed a poison arrow frog, they'd be dead within two or three minutes. But a Kodiak bear is six or eight times larger than a human, and they can eat almost anything. Not poison arrow frogs, though. It must have tasted bad, because the bear's reaction was immediate. With an ear-splitting, Chewbacca roar, it reared skywards, batting at its muzzle with its huge paws. For a moment it towered over me like a tree about to fall, then it twirled around and went charging away.

I jumped to my feet and dived into the basket.

I'd never given anyone an injection before, but they do it all the time on TV. Carefully breaking the top off the ampoule, I filled the syringe and injected the funnel-web antivenin into Jordan's arm.

JORDAN

It took them half an hour to get to us. First they had to deal with the bears. There was a heavy, metal grille that locked into place over the mouth of the den where the smaller bear had gone, and they sedated the larger one so the zoo vets could treat it for eating the poison arrow frog. It didn't die – it was a tough bear. Apparently they didn't use enough tranquilizer the first time, and it nearly bit one of the keepers. They told me this afterwards; I didn't see what happened. I wasn't interested. I sat in the bottom of the basket with Jordan cradled in my arms and Myrtle slobbering in my ear, and prayed that he was going to make it.

How long did it take for funnel-web antivenin to work? Was it too late to save him? Jordan showed no signs of recovery. Twice he had a series of muscular spasms that shook his whole body. Then his heart stopped again, and I had to give him CPR.

I could hear a lot of activity in the background – sirens, voices, the sound of vehicles coming and going. At one stage there were at least three helicopters buzzing around overhead. They made the lions roar in the next enclosure and caused a lot of shrieking, trumpeting and squawking from elsewhere in the zoo. Eventually someone must have told them to go away because they all flew off at the same time.

A woman with a megaphone called out to us, asking if we were all right, but I didn't feel like answering. I was a wreck. I had started to shake all over. It was partly delayed shock from everything that had happened, and partly because of Jordan. When you have little brothers – particularly identical twin little brothers – you don't have favorites, but Jordan was right up there. I might even have kissed him on the forehead a couple of times. But if I did, nobody saw.

Finally, I heard footsteps approaching. I thought it might be a bear – I didn't know yet what had happened to them – but part of me didn't even care because by now I was sure Jordan was going to die. But it wasn't a bear, it was two men – paramedics.

"G'day, mate," one of them said, trying to sound cheerful. "Which one of you has been bitten by the spider?"

It was pretty obvious, I thought. "Jordan," I said, sniffing back a tear.

The paramedic started climbing into the basket. "Okay, mate, give him to me."

I shook my head. I wasn't going to give Jordan up. If they wanted him taken to an ambulance, I would be the one who carried him.

"Come on, mate. We're here to help."

"It was my stupid fault," I sniveled, finally giving way to the tears I'd been holding back for half an hour. "The spider was on the two-way radio, and I flicked it in the air, and it landed on Jordan's head and bit him. And now he's –"

The rest of my words were drowned out by a loud, grunting roar from the next enclosure. Jordan's body gave a little twitch – as if he'd heard it, too. I looked down.

His eyes were wide-open!

"That sounded like a lion," Jordan whispered.

For a few seconds, I was too surprised to speak. I wiped my eyes, then nodded. "It was a lion," I said. "We're at the zoo."

"I thought we were going to the hospital."

"We are. But first we came to the zoo."

"Cool!" Jordan said weakly.

"Yeah, it is pretty cool. And now you'll get to ride in an ambulance."

Jordan's lips drew upwards into a tiny, trembling grin. "Harry will be jealous," he said.

ABOUT THE AUTHOR

Born in New Zealand, Justin D'Ath is one of twelve children. He came to Australia in 1971 to study for the missionary priesthood. After three years, he left the seminary in the dead of night and spent two years roaming Australia on a motorcycle. While doing that he began writing for motorcycle magazines. He published his first novel for adults in 1989. This was followed by numerous award-winning short stories, also for adults. Justin has worked in a sugar mill, on a cattle station, in a mine, on an island, in a laboratory, built cars, picked fruit, driven forklifts and taught writing for twelve years. He wrote his first children's book in 1996. To date he has published twenty-four books. He has two children, two grandchildren, and one dog.

www.justindath.com

Follow Sam on all of his
Extreme Adventures!

Book 1 – Crocodile Attack
Book 2 – Bushfire Rescue
Book 3 – Shark Bait
Book 4 – Scorpion Sting
Book 5 – Spider Bite
Book 6 – Man-Eater